凝煉知識品味閱讀

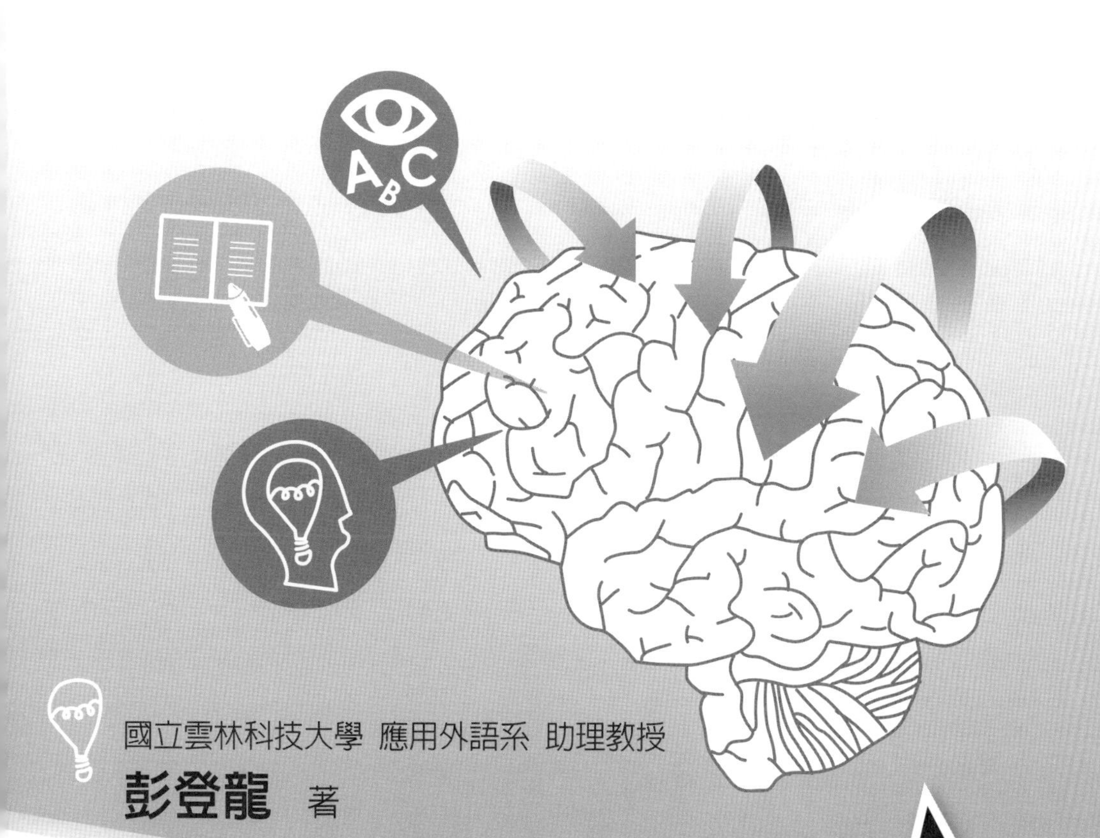

國立雲林科技大學 應用外語系 助理教授
彭登龍 著

高效的英文閱讀力

Efficient and Effective English Reading Comprehension

五南圖書出版公司 印行

序

PREFACE

對眾多學子而言，英文閱讀是大學與研究所學程中的必要課題，而如何有效率地閱讀英文原文書、英文文章或研究論文，實為當務之急。因此，唯有熟稔英文寫作原則與具備高效率的英文閱讀策略，才能以事半功倍之效，游刃有餘地悠遊於學海之中。

英文文章一般都有寫作傳統或規範可資遵循，包括各個段落裏的要素（主題句、闡述／發展句、結論句）、單一性原則、前後一致性……等原則。作者將其思想轉化為文字，而讀者則需運用寫作原則與閱讀文字來探索並解讀作者的原意。

編者在大學任教英文閱讀課時，深感學生因為不熟悉上述的寫作規範，以致於在面對英文原文書、英文文章或研究論文時，常因無法快速地掌握閱讀要領而倍感壓力。學生若能運用英文寫作原則與高效率的英文閱讀策略，應有助於提升其學習力。因此，編者收彙任教大學英文閱讀課程的上課內容、教學經驗和心得成書，分享快速掌握英文閱讀的訣竅，期望有助於讀者打造高效的英文閱讀力。

編者希望本書能為讀者精進英文閱讀技巧貢獻棉薄之力。惟編者才疏學淺，復因付梓匆促，書中難免有所疏漏或不當，尚祈各位先進與讀者不吝賜教。

國立雲林科技大學 應用外語系
彭登龍　助理教授

INTRODUCTION

【本書內容簡介】

本書共分為六章。第一章介紹英文書本的閱讀策略。第二章是英文文章的閱讀策略，強調英文文章三部曲，即序論（Introduction）、本文（Body Paragraphs）與結論（Conclusion）。第三章為英文段落的閱讀策略，重點在英文段落三部曲，即主題句（topic sentence）闡述／發展句（supporting / development sentences）與結論句（concluding sentences），另外介紹了英文段落各種組織類型，包括例證法／舉例法（exemplification）、時間順序法（chronological order）、空間順序法（spatial order）、類比法（analogy）、因果法（cause and effect）、比較或對比法（comparison or contrast）、分類法（classification）、定義法（definition）、過程分析法（process analysis）、主題法（topical organization）、推理法（inference）、問題解決法（problem-solution）、綜合法（combined methods）等。第四章是綜合練習，包含英文句子大意與主動詞的練習、英文段落練習、英文文章練習、一些考題的練習（如大學學測、大學指考、研究所考試、各類公職考試）。第五章係高層次的英文閱讀策略，包括布魯姆教育分類法（Bloom's Educational Taxonomy）、相互教學法（Reciprocal Teaching）、提問作者法（Questioning the Author）、SWOT分析法（SWOT Analysis）、主題結構分析（Topical Structure Analysis）。最後一章第六章為做筆記的策略，介紹了康乃爾筆記法（Cornell Note-taking Strategy）、心智圖法（Mind-mapping Strategy）與樹狀圖法（Tree Diagram Strategy）。

【本書重點導讀】

編者建議閱讀本書時，先掌握下列各章的重點，再參考本書的實例加以反覆練習，藉由熟能生巧，有效的增進閱讀力。

第一章　英文書本的閱讀策略 Reading Strategies for English Books

A. 注意作者名字及出版日期，先讀目錄頁及序言，並看一下書中圖表。

B. 瀏覽第一與最後一章之標題、圖表等。

C. 瀏覽中間的章節，再決定應該讀的章節。

D. 若有需要可先看一下書末的名詞解釋、主題索引、附錄。

第二章　英文文章的閱讀策略 Reading Strategies for English Articles

A Tri-part Structure of an Article

「文章三部曲」格式：IBC

Introduction（序論）、Body Paragraph(s)（本文）、Conclusion（結論）。

A. Introduction：thesis statement（文章的主旨）。

B. Body Paragraph(s)：main / central idea（每一段的大意）。

C. Conclusion: restatement of thesis statement（複述文章的主旨），paraphrase of main / central idea(s)（改寫本文當中的大意）。

Introduction	Thesis statement / position / stance / opinion / perspective
Body Paragraph(s)	Topic sentence (main / central idea) Supporting sentences Concluding sentence P.S. unity principle: only one single main idea in each body paragraph
Conclusion	1. Restatement of thesis statement / position / stance / opinion / perspective 2. Paraphrase of main / central idea(s)

第三章　英文段落的閱讀策略 Reading Strategies for English Paragraphs

A Tri-part Structure of a Body Paragraph

「段落三部曲」格式：TSC

Topic Sentence（主題句）、Supporting / Development Sentences（支持 / 發展句）、Concluding Sentence（結論句）。

A. Topic Sentence：main / central idea（中心思想或大意）。

B. Supporting / Development Sentences：supporting data, supporting evidence。

C. Concluding Sentence: paraphrase of main / central idea。

A tri-part structure of a body paragraph

Topic sentence (main / central idea).. **Supporting sentences** (e.g., exemplification, chronological order, spatial order, analogy, cause and effect, comparison or contrast, definition, classification, process analysis, problem-solution, inference, topical organization, a combination of different methods.......................................) **Concluding sentence** (e.g., in short, in summary, in brief...........................)

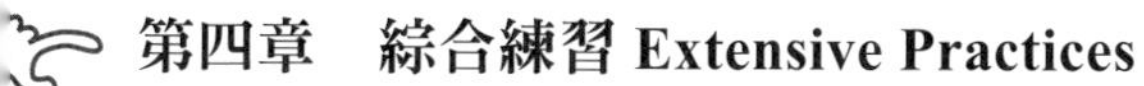

第四章　綜合練習 Extensive Practices

A.「文章三部曲」格式：IBC

Introduction（序論）、Body Paragraph(s)（本文）、Conclusion（結論）。

1. Introduction：文章的thesis statement。
2. Body Paragraph(s)：每一段的main / central idea。
3. Conclusion: 複述文章的thesis statement，改寫本文當中的main / central idea(s)。

B.「段落三部曲」格式：TSC

Topic Sentence（主題句）、Supporting / Development Sentences（支持 / 發展句）、Concluding Sentence（結論句）。

1. Topic Sentence：main / central idea（中心思想或大意）。
2. Supporting / Development Sentences：supporting data, supporting evidence。
3. Concluding Sentence: repeat main / central idea。

第五章　高層次的英文閱讀策略 Higher-order English Reading Strategies

A. Benjamin Bloom's Educational Taxonomy。

B. Reciprocal Teaching: Predicting, Questioning, Clarifying, Summarizing。

C. Questioning the Author。

D. SWOT Analysis: Strengths, Weaknesses, Opportunities, Threats。

E. TSA（Topical Structure Analysis): Parallel Progression, Sequential Progression, Extended Parallel Progression。

第六章　做筆記的策略 Note-taking Strategies

A. 康乃爾筆記法（Cornell Note-taking Strategy）。

B. 心智圖法 （Mind-mapping Strategy）。

C. 樹狀圖法（Tree-Diagram Strategy）。

目錄

CONTENTS

【第一章】

英文書本的閱讀策略

英文文章的閱讀策略

英文段落的閱讀策略

綜合練習

高層次的英文閱讀策略

做筆記的策略

前言

大學生時常需要閱讀英文原文書籍或文章，遇到不懂的單字時，就努力的查字典想查出中文翻譯，等到查完單字以後，卻又不清楚整段文字的大意，無論是英文本科系或非英文本科系的學生想必大都有這種經驗。而國際期刊有 80%；網路資訊更高達 85% 均以英文呈現，因此，如何在資訊與知識經濟的時代有效率的閱讀，並讀懂第一手的英文資訊，便成為具備高競爭力的現代知識經濟人所需具備的條件之一。有鑑於此，筆者彙集大學任教英文閱讀課時的上課內容、筆者的教學經驗和心得與讀者們分享，期望幫助學生在閱讀英文原文書時，能快速地掌握重點，以提升英文閱讀效率。

英文書本的閱讀策略

A. 注意作者名字及出版日期，先讀目錄頁及序言，並看一下書中圖表。

B. 瀏覽第一與最後一章之標題、圖表等。

C. 瀏覽中間的章節，再決定應該讀的章節。

D. 若有需要可先看一下書末的名詞解釋、主題索引、附錄。

先讀目錄頁時，就可對該書的內容有一初步認識，以下請看一個目錄頁（Contents or Table of Contents）的例子：

範例 目錄頁（**Contents or Table of Contents**）的例子 **1**

Contents

1. Introduction 1

Source: Larsen-Freeman, D. (2000). *Techniques and Principles in Language Teaching*. New York: Oxford University Press.

從上述的例子中，可以看出本書共有十二章，第一章是介紹，第二到第十一章是介紹各種英語教學法，而最後一章是結論，目錄頁編排非常的清楚。

以下請看另一個目錄頁（Contents or Table of Contents）的例子：

範例 目錄頁（Contents or Table of Contents）的例子 2

Contents

Source: Wells, G. (1999). *Dialogic inquiry: Toward a sociocultural practice and theory of education.* New York: Cambridge University Press.

從上述的例子中，可以看出本書共有十章，作者以三大部分為核心，第一部分為建立理論架構，底下有三章；第二部分為對話、學習、教學，底下有五章；第三部分為鄰近發展區中的學習與教學，底下有二章，也是一目了然。

在細讀序言文章之前，先讀主題句（通常為每一段的第一句），了解其中心思想（main / central idea）或大意，在序言中通常有一段（或數段）是介紹書本章節的安排與大概內容。以下舉一個序言（Introduction）例子如下：

範例 序言（**Introduction**）例子 **1**

1. Introduction

GOALS OF THIS BOOK

One of the **goals** of this book is for you to learn about many different language teaching methods....

A second goal is to help you uncover the thoughts....

A third goal is to introduce you to a variety of techniques....

LAYOUT OF CHAPTERS

Source: Larsen-Freeman, D. (2000). *Techniques and Principles in Language Teaching*. New York: Oxford University Press.

從上述的例子中，可以看出本書有三個目標，第一個目標就是讓讀者學習有關各種不同的語言教學方法，第二個目標是幫助讀者揭露引導教師自己行動的想法，第三個目標就是介紹讀者各式各樣的技巧。另外，可以看出章節的組織方式，以上序言的組織很清楚，使讀者很容易掌握閱讀的重點。

請看另一個序言（Introduction）的例子：

範例 序言（**Introduction**）例子 **2**

The book is arranged into **three parts**. **The first** establishes the theoretical framework.... **The second part** includes a number of classroom investigations.... **The final part** explores the significance of Vygotsky's construct of the "zone of proximal development....

Source: Wells, G. (1999). *Dialogic inquiry: Toward a sociocultural practice and theory of education.* New York: Cambridge University Press.

從上述的例子中，可以看出本書有三個部分，第一個部分是建立理論架構，第二個部分是介紹許多的教室觀察，第三個部分是探討維哥斯基鄰近發展區概念的重要性。接著，作者逐一介紹各個章節的重點，組織非常清楚。

請看最後一個序言（Introduction）的例子：

範例 序言（**Introduction**）例子 **3**

How...? We begin our enquiry (**Part 1**) by....In **Part 2** we will attempt to obtain.... These concepts are discussed in relation to one or several disciplines: linguistics (**Part 3**), anthropology, sociology and sociolinguistics (**Part 4**), psychology and psycholinguistics (**Part 5**), and educational theory (**Part 6**).

Source: Stern, H. H. (1996). *Fundamental concepts of language teaching.* Toronto: Oxford University Press. (p.3)

從上述的例子中，可以看出本書有六個部分，第一個部分是討論語言教學上一些常使用的名稱，第二個部分是獲得必要的歷史方向，第三個部分是語言學，第四個部分是人類學、社會學與社會語言學，第五個部分是心理學與心理語言學，第六個部分是教育理論，以關鍵字 parts 來安排，書本組織很清楚。

【第二章】

英文書本的閱讀策略

英文文章的閱讀策略

英文段落的閱讀策略

綜合練習

高層次的英文閱讀策略

做筆記的策略

前言

一般而言，英文文章不論有幾段，通常均由三部分組成，即第一段序論（Introduction）、中間段落為本文（Body Paragraphs）與最後一段結論（Conclusion）。為方便讀者記憶，編者稱之為文章三部曲（IBC）。在第一段中，作者或筆者會用一句話寫出 thesis statement（主旨句），亦即作者對某一主題的立場、意見或觀點（如持同意或不同意、贊成或反對、肯定或否定、正面或負面、積極或消極的看法），在本文的每段中說出中心想法或大意（main / central idea），而最後一段（結論段），作者需複述自己的立場，另外再複述或改寫本文中每段所提的大意。需注意的是，作者寫作時需符合二個主要原則：單一性（unity）原則與前後一致性（coherence）原則。單一性原則是指本文中的每段只能有一個大意；而前後一致性原則是指作者文章從頭到尾的立場要一致。

此外需注意的是，此章論述的三部曲不包括英文的其他文體（genre），例如小說、詩、散文等等。

文章三部曲

「文章三部曲」格式：IBC

Introduction（序論）、Body Paragraph(s)（本文）、Conclusion（結論）。

A. Introduction：文章的 thesis statement，通常是第一句。

B. Body Paragraph(s)：每一段的 main / central idea，通常是第一句。

C. Conclusion：複述文章的 thesis statement，改寫本文當中的 main / central idea(s)，通常是第一句或最後一句。

Introduction	Thesis statement / position / stance / opinion / perspective
Body Paragraph(s)	Topic sentence (main / central idea) Supporting / development sentences Concluding sentence P.S. unity principle: only one single main idea in each body paragraph
Conclusion	1. Restatement of thesis statement / position / stance / opinion / perspective 2. Paraphrase of main / central idea(s)

文章進行方式：

Introduction	Foretell 3 main ideas
Body Paragraph(s)	Tell 3 main ideas
Conclusion	Remind the readers what you have told them previously

文化思考模式

美國學者 Robert Kaplan 於 1966 年指出：不同的文化有不同的思考模式，因此每一個文化有其獨特的書寫組織方式。為了在不同文化間有效的溝通，我們需要了解不同語言的文化思考模式。因為這些文化思考模式會影響不同文化的人們口語與書面表達的方式，也會影響他們期望資訊呈現的方式。

以下為一個不同語言族群之不同文化模式的圖表，這個圖表並不是絕對的，但是可以視為培養跨文化溝通與文化知能的一個參考指引。

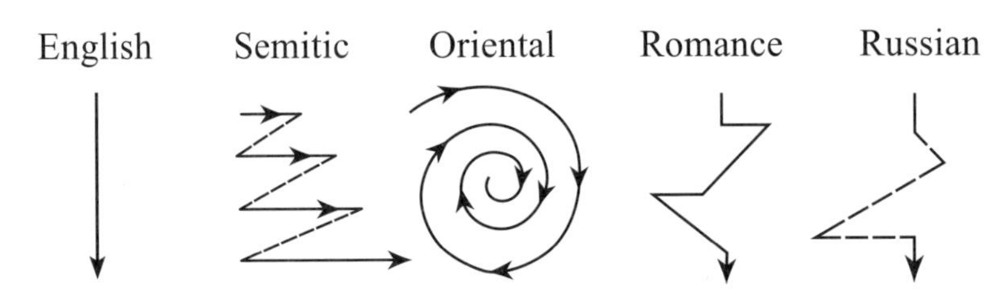

Source: Kaplan, R. (1966). Cultural thought patterns in intercultural education. *Language Learning*, 16, 1-20.

英文：（包括日耳曼語系的語言，如德語、荷蘭語、挪威語、丹麥語與瑞典語）溝通很直接，直線性發展，不偏離主題。

閃語：（例如阿拉伯語或希伯來語）思想以一系列平行的想法來表達，有正面的與反面的想法，同位語比附屬子句重要。

東方語：（亞洲語）溝通不直接，主題不直接提出，而是從各種不同的觀點考慮，旁敲側擊環繞主題。

羅曼語：（拉丁系語言，如法語、義大利語、羅馬尼亞語與西班牙語）溝通時常脫離主題，介紹無關的素材，能夠增加溝通的豐富性也可以。

俄語：像羅曼語一樣，俄語的溝通時常脫離主題。同時可能包括一系列的平行想法。

由以上的圖表中，我們可以看出中文與英文在寫作方面有很大的差異，那就是英文的寫作修辭模式是直線發展的，而中文是迂迴的。所以當我們在閱讀英文文章時，只要能掌握第一段的 thesis statement（即作者的主張、看法或意見），就可掌握全文的精髓，因為中間的段落，每一段的第一句有該段的主要大意（此為單一性 unity 原則），而最後一段作者會再複述其 thesis statement（此為前後一致性原則 coherence）。換言之，我們以作者寫作的方式來閱讀其文章，即可事半功倍地精準掌握文章的內涵。

文章範例

閱讀策略

1. 如果文章有標題的話，先看標題。
2. 快速掃描第一段以了解作者對此標題的看法。
3. 然後很快的掃描此文章（勿逐字閱讀），試圖了解本文的組織方式（如描述法、敘述法、例證法、時間法、空間法、因果法、比較或對比法、分類法、定義法、問題解決法、過程分析法、主題法、類比法、推理法、綜合法等等）。
4. 閱讀方式是——
   第一步驟：很快的掃描本文每一段的第一句，了解每段的大意。
   第二步驟：掃描全文看看是否有一直重複出現的單字、片語或同義字。
   第三步驟：很快的掃描本文中每一段的第一句與最後一句，每一段中間快速瀏覽。

A

Clinical depression is **a serious medical illness** that negatively affects how you feel, the way you think and how you act. Individuals with clinical depression are unable to function as they used to. Often they have lost interest in activities that were once enjoyable to them, and feel sad and hopeless for extended periods of time. Clinical depression is not the same as feeling sad or depressed for a few days and then feeling better. It can affect your body, mood, thoughts, and behavior. It can change your eating habits, your ability to work and study, and your interaction with people.

Clinical depression is not a sign of personal weakness, or a condition that can be willed away. In fact, it often interferes with a person's ability or will to get help. It is a serious illness that lasts for weeks, months and sometimes years. It may even influence someone to contemplate or attempt suicide.

People of all ages, genders, ethnicities, cultures, and religions can **suffer from** clinical depression. Each year it affects over 17 million American men and women (source: American Psychiatric Association). Clinical depression is frequently unrecognized and untreated. But, with the right treatment, most people who do seek help get better within several months. Many people begin to feel better in just a few weeks.

Source：99 年專門職業及技術人員普通考試導遊人員、領隊人員考試試題

文章分析

本文共三段。第一段為 Introduction，總共有六句，作者的 thesis statement（position, stance, opinion, perspective）是第一句，**Clinical depression** is a serious medical illness that negatively affects how you feel, the way you think and how you act.（臨床的沮喪是一種嚴重的醫學疾病，對於你的感覺、思考方式與行為會有負面的影響）。

然後第二到第三段的第一句均有談到 clinical depression。

以此文為例，本文屬於主題法（topical organization），亦即描述 clinical depression（臨床的沮喪），然後往下掃描，發現一直重複出現 clinical depression。

- **第一段：**

第一句以了解作者對此標題的看法「**Clinical depression** is a serious

medical illness that negatively affects how you feel, the way you think and how you act.」（臨床的沮喪是一種嚴重的醫學疾病，對於你的感覺、思考方式與行為會有負面的影響）。

- **第二段：**

第一句主題句點出本段大意「Clinical depression is not a sign of personal weakness, or a condition that can be willed away.」最後一句「It may even influence someone to contemplate or attempt suicide.」此段中間掃描看到「In fact, serious illness」。

- **最後一段：**

第一句「People of all ages, genders, ethnicities, cultures, and religions can suffer from clinical depression.」最後一句「Many people begin to feel better in just a few weeks.」此段中間掃描看到有數字「17 million American men and women」。

B

The Taiwanese **puppet show ("Budaixi")** is a distinguished form of performing arts in Taiwan. Although basically hand puppets, the figures appear as complete forms, with hands and feet, on an elaborately decorated stage.

The **puppet performance** is typically accompanied by a small orchestra. The backstage music is directed by the drum player. The drummer needs to pay attention to what is going on in the plot and follow the rhythm of the characters. He also uses the drum to conduct the other musicians. There are generally around four to five musicians who perform the backstage music. The form of music used is often associated with various performance techniques including acrobatics and skills like window-jumping, stage movement, and fighting. Sometimes unusual animal puppets also appear on stage for extra appeal, especially for children in the audience.

In general, **a show** needs two performers. The main performer is generally the chief or director of the troupe. He is the one in charge of the whole show, manipulating the main puppets, singing, and narrating. The supporting performer manipulates the puppets to coordinate with the main performer. He also changes the costumes of the puppets, and takes care of the stage. The relationship between the main performer and his partner is one of master and apprentice. Frequently, the master trains his sons to eventually succeed him as puppet masters.

Budaixi troupes are often hired to perform at processions and festivals held in honor of local gods, and on happy occasions such as weddings, births, and promotions. The main purpose of Budaixi is to worship and offer thanks to the deities. The shows also serve as a popular means of folk entertainment.

Source：101 年大學指考

文章分析

本文共四段。第一段為 Introduction，總共有二句，作者的 thesis statement（position, stance, opinion, perspective）是第一句，The Taiwanese puppet show（“Budaixi”）is a distinguished form of performing arts in Taiwan.（臺灣的布偶表演——布袋戲——在臺灣是一種卓越的表演藝術）。

然後第二到第三段的第一句均有談到 puppet performance, a show，最後一段第一句話 Budaixi troupes 係 puppet show 的同義詞。

以此文為例，本文屬於描述法（description），亦即描述布偶表演——布袋戲，然後往下掃描，發現一直重複出現 puppet performance, a show, Budaixi troupes。

- **第一段：**

  第一句以了解作者對此標題的看法「The Taiwanese puppet show ("Budaixi") is a distinguished form of performing arts in Taiwan.」（臺灣的布偶表演——布袋戲——在臺灣是一種卓越的表演藝術）。

- **第二段：**

  第一句「The **puppet performance** is typically accompanied by a small orchestra.」最後一句「Sometimes unusual animal puppets also appear on stage for extra appeal, especially for children in the audience.」此段中間掃描看到有鼓手與樂師「drum player, drummer, musicians」。

- **第三段：**

  第一句「In general, **a show** needs two performers.」最後一句「Frequently, the master trains his sons to eventually succeed him as puppet masters.」此段中間掃描看到有表演者「the main performer, the supporting performer」。

- **最後一段：**

  第一句「**Budaixi troupes** are often hired to perform at processions and festivals held in honor of local gods, and on happy occasions such as weddings, births, and promotions.」最後一句「The shows also serve as a popular means of folk entertainment.」此段中間掃描看到有目的「the purpose」。

C

The Fourth Factor

"Tell me how you used your sense of humor to defuse a difficult situation or teach an important lesson?" As a dean, I ask questions like that regularly when interviewing job candidates. In academe, we hire faculty members based on their teaching, research, and service, so I also ask a lot of questions about each of those facets of a candidate's career. **But there's a fourth factor that is important, too—attitude.**

I ask unusual questions during interviews to increase the likelihood that my university hires someone who, in addition to possessing significant knowledge and experience, has the **attitudes** that are essential to enhancing learning, teaching, and departmental culture on the campus. To get a glimpse into a candidate's character, I might ask the applicant to "describe your perfect day." One applicant sent to me after receiving high marks from the search committee responded, "I would sleep until noon and then lie in bed the rest of the day watching TV—I just subscribed to the 24-hour sports channel—and eating snack foods."

That answer triggered further inquiry into **the applicant's energy and motivational levels, his willingness to learn new things, and his ability to engage in meaningful interactions with others**. By the end of the interview, I was certain that he was not a good fit for our program. He was not offered the position.

It's not always so easy to make reliable and valid determinations about a candidate's **attitudes** in the short span of an interview. Fortunately, research with roots in the "perceptual psychology" work of the late Arthur W. Combs shows that effective educators possess discernable attitudes (Combs called them "perceptions" and used the term synonymously with "values, attitudes and beliefs") about themselves, students, and teaching.

Further, **those qualities** can be observed and measured during the interview process through the systematic use of carefully crafted questions. By listening thoughtfully to the answers, valuable insights can be garnered into how applicants perceive themselves, their students, and their chosen profession.

Source：96 學年度臺大碩士班招生考試試題

閱讀策略

1. 如果文章有標題的話，先看標題：The Fourth Factor（第四個因素）。
2. 快速掃描第一段以了解作者對此標題的看法：But there's a fourth factor that is important, too–attitude.（但是有第四個因素也很重要——態度）。
3. 然後很快的掃描此文章（勿逐字閱讀），試圖了解本文的組織方式。
4. 閱讀方式是——

   第一步驟：很快的掃描本文每一段的第一句，了解每段的大意。

   第二步驟：掃描全文看看是否有一直重複出現的單字、片語或同義字。

   第三步驟：很快的掃描本文每一段的第一句與最後一句，每一段中間快速瀏覽。

文章分析

本文共五段。第一段為 Introduction，總共有四句，作者的 thesis statement (position, stance, opinion, perspective）是第四句，But there's a fourth factor that is important, too–attitude.（但是有第四個因素也很重要——態度）。讀者可能會問，為什麼不是其他句子，如果各位讀者往文章下面每一段的第一句話，發現作者一直談到態度（第二段第一句 attitudes；第三段第一句 the applicant's energy and motivational levels；第四段第一句 those qualities），以上這些關鍵字均是 attitude 的同義字或詞，故作者的立場是第四句，換言之，作者認為態度很重要。

一般情形下，作者的立場或想法是第一段的第一句，但是遇到有轉折字或片語（如 But, However, In fact As a matter of fact...）時，則作者的意見通常在以上這些轉折字或片語之後。

以此文為例，本文屬於主題法（topical organization），亦即作者針對態度此主題加以說明其重要性，並談到在面談過程中，觀察與測量申請工作者的態度之方法。

- **第一段：**

  第四句以了解作者對此標題的看法「But there's a fourth factor that is important, too–attitude.」（但是有第四個因素也很重要——態度）。

- **第二段：**

  第一句「I ask unusual questions during interviews to increase the likelihood that my university hires someone who, in addition to possessing significant knowledge and experience, has the **attitudes** that are essential to enhancing learning, teaching, and departmental culture on the campus.」

  最後一句「One applicant sent to me after receiving high marks from the search committee responded, "I would sleep until noon and then lie in bed the rest of the day watching TV - I just subscribed to the 24-hour sports channel - and eating snack foods."」此段中間掃描看到有「To get a glimpse into a candidate's character, I might ask the applicant to "describe your perfect day."」。

- **第三段：**

第一句「That answer triggered further inquiry into **the applicant's energy and motivational levels, his willingness to learn new things, and his ability to engage in meaningful interactions with others.**」最後一句「He was not offered the position.」此段中間掃描看到「By the end of the interview....」。

- **第四段：**

第一句「It's not always so easy to make reliable and valid determinations about a candidate's **attitudes** in the short span of an interview.」最後一句「Fortunately, research with roots in the "perceptual psychology" work of the late Arthur W. Combs shows that ....」。

- **最後一段：**

第一句「Further, **those qualities** can be observed and measured during the interview process through the systematic use of carefully crafted questions.」最後一句「By listening thoughtfully to the answers, valuable insights can be garnered into how applicants perceive themselves, their students, and their chosen profession.」。

【第三章】

前言

一般而言，英文段落中，通常由三部分組成，即所謂的段落三部曲，即第一句主題句（topic sentence）、支持或發展句（supporting or development sentences）、與最後一句結論句（concluding sentence）。

段落三部曲

「段落三部曲」格式：TSC

Topic Sentence（主題句）、Supporting / Development Sentences（支持 / 發展句）、Concluding Sentence（結論句）。

A. Topic Sentence: main / central idea（中心思想或大意）。

B. Supporting / Development Sentences: supporting data, supporting evidence。

C. Concluding Sentence: paraphrase of main / central idea。

英文段落的閱讀策略

在細讀文章之前，先讀主題句（topic sentence，通常為每一段的第一句），了解其中的中心思想或大意（main / central / controlling idea），再分析其闡述句 / 發展句（supporting / development sentences）中所運用的技巧，例如：例證法 / 舉例法（exemplification）、時間順序法（chronological order）、空間順序法（spatial order）、類比法（analogy）、因果法（cause and effect）、比較或對比法（comparison or contrast）、分類法（classification）、定義法（definition）、過程分析法（process analysis）、主題法（topical organization）、推理法（inference）、問題解決法（problem-solution）、綜合法（combined methods）等，譬如在時間順序法的文章中會讀到時間副詞（如：年代、first, second / then, third, finally 等），而在空間順序法的文章中會看到方位或地方副詞（如：east, west, south, north），最後了解該段的結論句（通常為每一段的最後一句）。

所以，欲了解一段文章的大意，只須先清楚主題句中的中心思想或大意的關鍵字（key words），若遇有不懂的單字，將其查出，至於段落中不懂的單字可依字源學的概念：即字根（word root / stem 字的意義）、字首（prefix 肯定 / 否定 / 方向 / 位置）、字尾（suffix 詞性：名詞 / 動詞 / 形容詞 / 副詞）與語境 / 前後文（context）來猜測即可，不用花費太多的時間查出每個不懂的單字。另外要注意的是，英文段落中通常只有一個中心思想或大意，此即為 unity（單一性）原則。英文段落的架構，以圖表的樣子呈現，有如下圖：

Topic sentence (including main / central idea; it's usually the first sentence in a body paragraph)....。**Supporting sentences** (exemplification, chronological order, spatial order, analogy, cause and effect, comparison and contrast, classification, definition, process analysis, topical organization, inference, problem-solution, or a combination of different methods)。**Concluding sentence** (summary of the whole paragraph)....。

一般而言，段落中間是支持或發展句（supporting evidence, data），用來支持主題句中的大意，常用的方法有舉例、證據、數字、統計、引用專家的說法、事實等等。具體而言，共有下列方法：例證法 / 舉例法（exemplification）、時間順序法（chronological order）、空間順序法（spatial order）、類比法（analogy）、因果法（cause and effect）、比較或對比法（comparison or contrast）、分類法（classification）、定義法（definition）、過程分析法（process analysis）、主題法（topical organization）、推理法（inference）、問題解決法（problem-solution）、綜合法（combination of different methods）等等策略，而學術上最常用的就是第一種例證法 / 舉例法（exemplification）。

找英文段落大意的方法

以下的萬用句型（generic sentence pattern）可以幫助讀者快速找到英文的主詞、動詞、受詞或補語。

英文一般皆有主詞 + 動詞的基本要素。大意一定是內容字（content words），如主詞動詞、受詞或補語，不會是功能字（function words）如 the / a / an 或修飾語（adj.）介詞片語、形容詞子句。

The	Prep. Phrase (of the....)
A + (adj.) + N. (**S.**) +	adj. Clause (who / which + S. V.) + **V.** (+ **O.** / **C.**)
An	P.P. (-ed)
	V + ing

中英翻譯時應注意原則：

基本上，中文是意合語言，句子比較短；而英文是形合語言，因常有後位修飾語（如以上句型介系詞片語、形容詞子句），所以句子比較長。

1. 增譯：有時需增加翻譯。
2. 減譯：有時需減少翻譯。
3. 詞性轉換：有時需詞性轉換，例如名詞、動詞、形容詞、副詞、介詞需轉換。
4. 主、被動句互換：有時需主動句與被動句互換。
5. 重新組織整理：總而言之，翻譯時需重新組織整理，以符合中英文的習慣語法或用法。

以下以一段落為例，說明英文段落的閱讀策略：

The **city of Brisbane** in Australia has many **wonderful attractions. Firstly,** the most notable tourist attraction is the Gold Coast, the surfer's paradise. **Secondly**, Brisbane has many good restaurants, because of its sea food and culturally diverse immigrants. **Finally**, Queen Street Mall offers enjoyable shopping centers for visitors. **In summary, these elements** make **Brisbane a very attractive city** for tourists.

1. The city of Brisbane in Australia has many wonderful attractions. 主詞為 city，動詞為 has。
2. Firstly, the most notable tourist attraction is the Gold Coast. 主詞為 tourist attraction，動詞為 is。
3. Secondly, Brisbane has many good restaurants, because of its sea food and culturally diverse immigrants. 主詞為 Brisbane，動詞為 has。
4. Finally, Queen Street Mall offers enjoyable shopping centers for visitors. 主詞為 Queen Street Mall，動詞為 offers。
5. In summary, these elements make Brisbane a very attractive city for tourists. 主詞為 elements，動詞為 make。

- **主題句：**The city of Brisbane in Australia has many wonderful attractions.
- **中心思想或大意（關鍵字）：**關鍵字 the city of Brisbane，many wonderful attractions. 大意是布里斯本市有許多吸引人之處。
- **闡述句策略：**依重要順序（order of importance）舉出 Gold Coast, restaurants, Queen Street Mall 三個例子來說明。
- **結論句：**In summary, these elements make Brisbane a very attractive city for tourists.
- **中心思想或大意（關鍵字）：**關鍵字 elements。

- **大意：**澳洲布里斯本市有許多吸引人之處。接著，作者用例證法(1)黃金海岸；(2)許多餐廳；(3)皇后街購物中心等三個例子來闡述其中心思想。最後，作者以結論句來改寫（paraphrase）總結三個例子，摘要總結布里斯本市對觀光客而言是一個非常具有吸引力的城市。

以上的段落也可以改寫成其他的都市，可用來介紹某一城市，例如：

The **city of Taipei** in Taiwan has many **wonderful attractions. Firstly,** the most notable site is the tall and majestic 101 high-rise building, which is often referred to as Taipei 101. **Secondly,** Taipei has many famous night markets, such as Shilin Night Market and Shida Night Market, two favorite places for quick snack and shopping. **Finally,** the National Palace Museum, an art museum in Taipei city, has a permanent collection of 693,507 pieces of ancient Chinese artifacts and artworks, making it one of the largest in the world. In addition, the museum houses several treasured items that are the pride of their collection and famous worldwide. **In summary, these elements** make **Taipei a very attractive city** for tourists.

以下以另一段落為例，說明英文段落的閱讀策略：

Because Americans are a blend of people from many countries, there are only **a few characteristics** that apply to all Americans. Perhaps the most basic of these is **American individuality** that is evident in their history from the days of their founding fathers. The second characteristic shared by all Americans is **their paradoxical combination of idealism and practicality**. Another typically American feature is **the emphasis**

they place on money and the things it can buy-that is, the materialism. Finally, in practically all American families, **their parents exert less influence on them** than do parents in other parts of the world. These **elements** are deeply embedded in the American character, but Americans are subject to change in a relatively short period of time.

Source：94 年專門職業及技術人員普通考試導遊人員、領隊人員考試試題

- **主題句：**Because Americans are a blend of people from many countries, there are only a few characteristics that apply to all Americans.
- **中心思想或大意（關鍵字）：**關鍵字 a few characteristics 大意是一些特點。
- **闡述句策略：**依序舉出 American individuality, paradoxical combination of idealism and practicality, the emphasis they place on money, their parents exert less influence on them 四個特點。
- **結論句：**These elements are deeply embedded in the American character, but Americans are subject to change in a relatively short period of time.
- **大意：**美國人是由許多國家的人民混合而成，但只有一些特點適用於所有的美國人。

文章段落各種類型整理

接著各以幾個段落，介紹各種不同類型的闡述句或發展句中所運用的技巧：

一、例證法 / 舉例法（Exemplification）

所謂例證法，就是使用例子來說明要討論的立場、主張、觀點或意見，這是最常見也是最有效的說明文。

We can **harness energy** from the sun, or solar energy, in many ways. **For instance**, many satellites in space are equipped with large panels whose solar cells transform sunlight directly into electric power. These panels are covered with glass and are painted black inside to absorb as much heat as possible.

Source：99 年大學指考

- **主題句：**We can harness energy from the sun, or solar energy, in many ways.
- **中心思想（關鍵字）：**harness energy。
- **發展句策略：**例證法（for instance）。
- **結論句：**N / A（Not Applicable）。
- **大意：**我們可以用許多方式從太陽或太陽能利用能源。接著作者以例證法說明。

【例證法 / 舉例法】常用字 / 片語：

for example, for instance, in this case, in another case, on this occasion, in this situation, take the case of, proof of this, evidence of this, thus, in this manner, in other words., such as, that is, case, specifically, generally, as proof, as follows, as below, to name a few, to be specific。

二、時間順序法（Chronological Order）

所謂時間順序法，就是以時間的先後順序（如年代、西元年）來說明人物或事件發展的經過。

Doctor of Philosophy, usually abbreviated as PhD or Ph.D., is an **advanced academic degree** awarded by universities. The first Doctor of Philosophy degree was awarded in Paris in **1150**, but the degree did not acquire its modern status until the early **19th century**. The doctorate of philosophy as it exists today originated at Humboldt University. The German practice was later adopted by American and Canadian universities, eventually becoming common in large parts of the world in **the 20th century**.

Source：100 年大學指考

- **主題句：**Doctor of Philosophy, usually abbreviated as PhD or Ph.D., is an advanced academic degree awarded by universities.
- **中心思想（關鍵字）：**Doctor of Philosophy, advanced academic degree。
- **發展句策略：**時間順序法（1150, the 19th century, the 20th century）。
- **結論句：**The German practice was later adopted by American and Canadian universities, eventually becoming common in large parts of the world in the 20th century.
- **大意：**哲學博士通常縮寫成 PhD 或 Ph.D.，是大學所頒發的高級學位。接著作者以時間順序法說明哲學博士學位的普及經過情形。

【時間順序法】常用字 / 片語：
年 / 年代, first, second, etc., at once, immediately, meanwhile, in the meantime, at the same time, after an interval, presently, somewhat later, soon, then, next, now, later, finally, eventually, thereupon, thereafter, after, afterwards, in the end, at last, at length, in the interim, then。

三、空間順序法（Spatial Order）

所謂空間順序法，就是以空間位置（如國家、地區、東西南北、前後左右）來說明人或物的相互關係。

Vancouver Island is one of the most beautiful places in the world. It is situated off the west coast of Canada, about one and a half hour by ferry from Vancouver on the mainland. Victoria, the capital city, was founded over one hundred and fifty years ago and is famous for its old colonial style buildings and beautiful harbor. It is the center of government for the province of British Columbia, so many of the people living there are employed as public servants. The lifestyle is very relaxed, compared to other cities in Canada, and this is attracting a lot of people to move there after they retire. The island is also popular with tourists because of the magnificent mountain scenery and the world-renowned Butchart Gardens.

Source：101 年專門職業及技術人員普通考試導遊人員、領隊人員考試試題

- **主題句：**Vancouver Island is one of the most beautiful places in the world.
- **中心思想（關鍵字）：**Vancouver Island。
- **發展句策略：**空間順序法（west coast, Vancouver, Victoria, British Columbia, Butchart Gardens）。
- **結論句：**The island is also popular with tourists because of the magnificent mountain scenery and the world-renowned Butchart Gardens.
- **大意：**溫哥華島是世界上最美麗的地方之一。接著作者以空間法描述溫哥華島。

【空間順序法】常用字 / 片語：

國名，地名, above, across from, adjacent to, also, around, at the same place, before, below, beneath, beyond, close to, down, further, here, there, in front of, in the distance, nearby, next to, near, on the left, on the right, on top of, opposite to, over, under, up。

四、類比法（Analogy）

所謂類比法，就是利用相似概念，以比較具體或易了解的事物或過程，來解釋較抽象與較難理解的事物或過程，這是一種特殊的比較法。下面的文章段落將 swarm intelligence 與 how social animals like ants and bees behave in a crowd 以類比法說明，此法很有效，因為可幫助讀者想像看見看不到的東西，相較 swarm intelligence，social animals like ants and bees 的概念比較熟悉而具體。

Researchers on customer behavior are now investigating how **"swarm intelligence"** (that is, how **social animals like ants or bees** behave in a crowd) can be used to influence what people buy. The idea is that, if a certain product is seen to be popular, shoppers are likely to choose it too. With the help of modern technology, some supermarkets are now able to keep customers informed about what others are buying. As a customer walks past a shelf of goods in one of these supermarkets, a screen on the shelf will tell him how many people currently in the store have chosen that particular product. As it turns out, such a "swarm moves" model increases sales without the need to give people discounts. The reason is simple: it gives **shoppers** the satisfaction of knowing that they bought the "right" product-that is, the one everyone else bought.

Source：96 年大學指考

- **主題句：**Researchers on customer behavior are now investigating how "swarm intelligence" (that is, how social animals like ants or bees behave in a crowd) can be used to influence what people buy.
- **中心思想（關鍵字）：**swarm intelligence, how social animals like ants or bees behave in a crowd。
- **闡述句策略：**類比法（swarm intelligence, social animals, shoppers）。
- **結論句：**無。
- **大意：**調查客戶行為的研究人員正在調查群集智慧如何被使用來影響人們購買什麼東西（換言之，像螞蟻或蜜蜂的社會性動物在群集中的行為方式）。接著作者以類比法說明 shoppers 與群集智慧（swarm intelligence）。

【類比法】常用字 / 片語：
like, as, 明喻（simile，即句中有 like, as 字眼）。
暗 / 隱喻（metaphor，即句中無 like, as 字眼）。
Our life is like a journey（明喻）。
Our life is a journey（暗 / 隱喻）。

五、因果法（Cause and Effect）

所謂因果法，就是以因果（cause and effect）關係的方式闡述文章段落（例如通常大多在回答 why 之類的問題）。

Jet lag, **caused by** traveling between time zones, is becoming a common problem for frequent travelers: for 49 per cent it is only a nuisance and for 45 percent it is a real problem. It **is caused by** disruption to the internal biological clock, and may lead to digestive problems, tiredness, and sleep disruption.

Generally speaking, our biological clock is slightly disturbed if we just move into the next time zone, but jet lag becomes a problem once we have passed through three or four time zones. The body takes about one day to get over each hour of time difference. But the seriousness of jet lag problems also depends on our direction of travel. If we go north or south, we won't notice any difference, **because** there is usually no time zone change. However, if we travel west we will be in advance of ourselves as far as our internal clock is concerned, and problems may arise. A west-to-east journey, on the other hand, makes us late compared to the local time. It often demands even greater effort in adjustment since we are not quick enough to catch up with the new time schedule. Therefore, a trip from New York to Los Angeles often **causes** fewer problems than a Los Angeles-New York trip.

Source：94 年大學學測

- **主題句：**Jet lag, caused by traveling between time zones, is becoming a common problem for frequent travelers: for 49 per cent it is only a nuisance and for 45 percent it is a real problem.
- **中心思想（關鍵字）：**jet lag。
- **闡述句策略：**因果法（is caused by, because）。
- **結論句：**Therefore, a trip from New York to Los Angeles often causes

fewer problems than a Los Angeles-New York trip.

- **大意：**時差對於時常旅行的人而言，愈來愈成為一個普遍的問題，時差是因為在不同時區之間旅行所引起的。接著作者以因果法說明時差是因對內在生理時鐘產生干擾所引起。
- **註：**產生或導致的同義詞有 cause, lead to, give rise to, contribute to, result in, yield, generate, bring about 等等。結果的同義詞有 result from, as a result, as a concequence, consequently。

【因果法】常用字 / 片語：

Reasons（原因）：because, since, for, as, in that, in the sense that, in as much as, for the reason that。

Result（結果）：as a result of, accordingly, thus, consequently, hence, therefore, wherefore, thereupon, so, it follows that, one may infer, one may conclude。

六、比較或對比法（Comparison or Contrast）

所謂比較法，是找出兩種或兩種以上的人、事、物（例如兩種學生：大學生與移民小孩）的相似性（similarities）；而對比法，則是找出兩種或兩種以上的人、事、物（例如不同作家或其做法 / 想法）的相異性（differences）。

1. 比較法（相似性 similarities）

Recent studies show that **levels of happiness** for most people **change** throughout their lives. In a British study between 1991 and 2003, people were asked how satisfied they are with their lives. The resulting statistics graph shows a smile-shaped curve. Most of the people start off happy and become progressively **less happy** as they grow older. For many of them, the most miserable period in their life is their 40s. After that, their levels of happiness climb. Furthermore, it seems that **men** are **slightly happier** on average than **women** in their teens, but women bounce back and overtake men later in life. The low point seems to last longer for women-throughout their 30s and 40s, only climbing once women reach 50. Men, on the other hand, have the lowest point in their 40s, going up again when they reach 50.

Source：96 年大學指考

- **主題句：**Recent studies show that levels of happiness for most people change throughout their lives.
- **中心思想（關鍵字）：**levels of happiness change。
- **闡述句策略：**比較法（less happy, man vs. women, slightly happier, on the other hand）。
- **結論句：**N / A。
- **大意：**最近的研究顯示，對於大部分的人們來說，幸福的層次在一生當中會改變。接著作者以比較法比較男士與女士在人生不同階段幸福層次的改變情形。

【比較法】常用字 / 片語：

形容詞比較級（e.g., more, less, higher, lower...etc.）

parallel to, similar to, have much in common, similarly, likewise, in like manner, another, equally, equally important, on the same grounds, in a similar vein, by the same token, besides, in fact, both, also, furthermore, too, then, in addition to, in the same way, just as...so, moreover, at the same time, accordingly, however, whereas, while, but, on the other hand, except, by comparison, when compared to, in comparison with, up against, balanced against, vis-à-vis。

2. 對比法（相異性 **differences**）

Solar energy has a lot to offer. To begin with, it is a clean fuel. **In contrast,** fossil fuels, such as oil or coal, release harmful substances into the air when they are burned. What's more, fossil fuels will run out, but solar energy will continue to reach the Earth long after the last coal has been mined and the last oil well has run dry.

Source：99 年大學指考

- **主題句：**Solar energy has a lot to offer.
- **中心思想（關鍵字）：**solar energy。
- **發展句策略：**對比法（In contrast）。
- **結論句：**N / A。
- **大意：**太陽能有很多好處。接著作者以對比法對比太陽能與化石燃料（如石油或煤）說明太陽能的好處。

【對比法】常用字 / 片語：
by contrast, but, on the contrary, on the other hand, despite, different from, in spite of, another, instead, whereas, nevertheless, still, however, rather, yet, after all, for all of that, on the contrary, notwithstanding, in contrast。
not only...but also, years ago...today, the earlier...the later, the

first...whereas the second, on the one hand...on the other hand, here...there, this...that, then...now, some...others, once...now。

七、分類法（Classification）

所謂分類法，就是將人事物依其特色分成不同類別（例如將照相機依功能特點分成傳統相機與數位相機）。

Generally there are **two ways** to name typhoons: the **number-based convention** and **the list-based convention**. Following the **number-based convention**, typhoons are coded with various types of numbers such as a 4-digit or a 6-digit code. For example, the 14th typhoon in 2003 can be labeled either as Typhoon 0314 or Typhoon 200314. The disadvantage of this convention, however, is that a number is hard to remember. The **list-based convention**, on the other hand, is based on the list of typhoon names compiled in advance by a committee, and is more widely used.

Source：101 年大學學測

- **主題句：**Generally there are two ways to name typhoons: the number-based convention and the list-based convention.
- **中心思想（關鍵字）：**two ways to name typhoons。
- **發展句策略：**分類法（the number-based convention, the list-based convention）。
- **結論句：**N / A。
- **大意：**一般而言，命名颱風有二種方式：以數字為基礎的傳統與以名單為基礎的傳統。接著作者以分類法說明颱風命名的二種方式。

【分類法】常用字 / 片語：
types, kinds, groups, classes, sorts, sources, categories, varieties, clusters, directions, classify, divide...into..., break...into..., fall into...。

八、定義法（Definition）

所謂定義法，即針對某一專業術語的概念加以定義。通常用於專有名詞的領域。

Oniomania is the technical term for the compulsive desire to shop, more commonly **referred to as** compulsive shopping or shopping addiction. Victims often experience feelings of contentment when they are in the process of purchasing, which seems to give their life meaning while letting them forget about their sorrows. Once leaving the environment where the purchasing occurred, the feeling of a personal reward would be gone. To compensate, the addicted person would go shopping again. Eventually a feeling of suppression will overcome the person. For example, cases have shown that the bought goods will be hidden or destroyed, because the person concerned feels ashamed of their addiction and tries to conceal it. He or she is either regretful or depressed. In order to cope with the feelings, the addicted person is prompted to turn to another purchase.

Source：98 年大學指考

- **主題句：**Oniomania is the technical term for the compulsive desire to shop, more commonly referred to as compulsive shopping or shopping addiction.
- **中心思想（關鍵字）：**oniomania, compulsive shopping, shopping addition。
- **闡述句策略：**定義法（referred to）。
- **結論句：**N / A。
- **大意：**Oniomania 是一個專有名詞，指的是強迫的購買欲望，通常被稱為強迫購買與購買成癮。接著作者以定義法說明其成因。

【定義法】常用字 / 片語：

term, define, refer to, mean, sense, denote, be described as, be defined as, be seen as, be considered (to be), be thought of as, be known as, be called / named / termed as, be taken to be as, to be referred to as, be viewed as。

九、過程分析法（Process Analysis）

所謂過程分析法，即說明一件事情如何從開始到完成的各個步驟或階段（例如 first, next, then, later, finally），通常是回答 how to 的問題。

Demolition is the tearing-down of buildings and other structures. You can level a five-story building easily with excavators and wrecking balls, but when you need to bring down a 20-story skyscraper, explosive demolition is the preferred method for safely demolishing the huge structure.

In order to demolish a building safely, blasters must map out a careful plan ahead of time. **The first step** is to examine architectural blueprints of the building to determine how the building is put together. **Next**, the blaster crew tours the building, jotting down notes about the support structure on each floor. **Once** they have gathered all the data they need, the blasters devise a plan of attack. They decide what explosives to use, where to position them in the building, and how to time their explosions.

Generally speaking, blasters will explode the major support columns on the lower floors first and then on a few upper stories. In a 20-story building, the blasters might blow the columns on the first and second floor, as well as the 12th and 15th floors. In most cases, blowing the support structures on the lower floors is sufficient for collapsing the building, but loading explosives on upper floors helps break the building material into smaller pieces as it falls. This makes for easier cleanup following the blast. The main challenge in bringing a building down is controlling the direction in which it falls. To topple the building towards the north, the blasters set off explosives on the north side of the building first. By controlling the way it collapses, a blasting crew will be able to tumble the building over on one side, into a parking lot or other open area. This sort of blast is the easiest to execute, and it is generally the safest way to go.

Source：101 年大學指考

- **主題句：**Demolition is the tearing-down of buildings and other structures.
- **中心思想（關鍵字）：**demolition。
- **闡述句策略：**過程分析法（The first step, next, Once..., the blasters....）。

- **結論句：**This sort of blast is the easiest to execute, and it is generally the safest way to go.
- **大意：**破壞就是將建築物與其他的結構拆除下來。接著作者以過程分析法（The first step, next, Once...）依序介紹拆除建築物的過程。

【過程分析法】常用字 / 片語：

to begin with, first of all, stage, procedure, steps, process, first, second, etc., but, finally, also, another, yet, once, such, then, thus, as a result, at last, consequently, for example, for instance, in addition, in this case, otherwise, in closing, now, for this purpose, furthermore, moreover, likewise, next, on the contrary, in summary, on the other hand, in conclusion, therefore。

Sequence（順序）：

first, second, third, A, B, C, 1, 2, 3, next, then, following, this, at this time, now, at this point, after, afterward, after this, subsequently, soon, finally, consequently, before this, previously, preceding this, simultaneously, concurrently, at this time, therefore, hence。

十、主題法（Topical Organization）

所謂主題法，是依作者想要闡述的主題（subject matter）本質呈現的方法，通常對於一些比較熟悉的題目會使用此方法（例如 disease, financial reports, democratic institutions, policy issues）。

The link between conditions in the womb and breast cancer is very surprising. The very existence of the disease is bad enough. What terrifies women is that it strikes so many who have no known factor–such as age, close relatives with the disease or not bearing a child before 30. Dr. Karin Michels of the Harvard School of Public Health has identified one overlooked cause. After collecting health data from tens of thousands of nurses, Michels and colleagues reported in 1997 that women who had weighed about 5.5 pounds at birth had half the risk of breast cancer compared with women who had weighed about 9 pounds at birth. That was especially true of breast cancer in women aged 50 or younger. "There is increasing evidence," says Michels, "that breast cancer may originate before birth."

Source：99 年公務人員特種考試外交領事人員及國際新聞人員考試

- **主題句：**The link between conditions in the womb and breast cancer is very surprising.
- **中心思想（關鍵字）：**breast cancer。
- **闡述句策略：**主題法（breast cancer）。
- **結論句：**"There is increasing evidence," says Michels, "that breast cancer may originate before birth."
- **大意：**子宮的情況與乳癌之間的關係令人非常驚訝。接著作者以主題法說明乳癌可能發源於出生之前。

【主題法】常用字 / 片語：
各種不同領域的主題，例如醫學、財政、生物、語言學……等等。

十一、推理法（Inference）

所謂推理法，就是作者未使用明確的方法闡述中心思想，需要讀者閱讀完文章段落後，再經由文章的說明所獲致的認知與推論之方法。換言之，就是讀者要領悟言外之意（read between the lines）。

Researchers now warn that the **supply of PhDs has far outstripped demand**. America produced more than 100,000 doctoral degrees between 2005 and 2009, while there were just 16,000 new professorships. **In research**, the story is similar. Even graduates who find work outside universities may not fare all that well. **Statistics** show that five years after receiving their degrees, more than **60%** of PhDs in **Slovakia** and more than **45%** in Belgium, the Czech Republic, Germany, and **Spain** are still on temporary contracts. About one-third of Austria's PhD graduates take jobs unrelated to their degrees.

Which of the following **may be inferred** from the third paragraph?

(A) PhD graduates in Austria are not encouraged to work outside university.

(B) Most German PhDs work at permanent jobs immediately after graduation.

(C) It is much easier for American PhD holders to find a teaching position than a research job.

(D) It is more difficult for PhDs to get a permanent job five years after graduation in Slovakia than in Spain.

【Answer】(D)

Source：100 年大學指考

主題句：Researchers now warn that the supply of PhDs has far outstripped demand.

- **中心思想（關鍵字）：**supply of PhDs has far outstripped demand。
- **闡述句策略：**推理法（In research, Statistics）。
- **結論句：**N / A。
- **大意：**研究人員現在警告說博士的供給遠遠超過需求。斯洛伐克有60%，而西班牙有 45% 畢業後五年現在仍是暫時合約的情形，由此推論，斯洛伐克的博士比西班牙的博士更難獲得永久的職業。

【推理法】常用字 / 片語：

infer, reason, inference, what can we inferred, what can be inferred from...。

十二、問題解決法（Problem - Solution）

所謂問題解決法，就是作者先提出問題，再說明解決之道的方法（例如 problem, solution）。

Japan is dealing with a **problem** that's just starting to sweep the world-an **aging population** combined with a **shrinking work force**. Therefore, aged Japanese are now being encouraged to work longer in life. By so doing, it is hoped that Japan's government will save its increasingly burdened pension (i.e., payment received after retirement) system from going bankrupt. In 2000, the Japanese could get a full pension from the government at 60. But by 2025, they won't get any until they are 65. What's more, premiums paid by workers every month are set to rise while payouts they get after retirement fall.

To help workers to **cope with** this, Japan passed a law last year that requires companies by 2013 to raise their retirement age from 60 to 65 or rehire their retired workers. The new policy could be a strain for employers. In a country where forced layoffs are a last resort, large companies traditionally have relied on retirement to reduce payrolls. They were just about to enjoy a big cut in personnel costs because of the mass retirement of Japan's baby boomers. These people born between 1947 and 1949 make up 5.2 million members of the work force. Consequently, there was much opposition from corporations to the new retirement law. Early signs suggest that large corporations will hesitate in raising their retirement ages. And, unlike the U.S., Japan has no law against discrimination based on age. Violators of the new law would face only "administrative guidance," not penalties. Such resistance is hurting the effectiveness of the policies, which may thus **prolong the aging problem**.

Source：96 年大學指考

- **主題句：**Japan is dealing with a problem that's just starting to sweep the world-an aging population combined with a shrinking work force.
- **中心思想（關鍵字）：**problem, aging population, shrinking work force。
- **闡述句策略：**問題解決法（cope with）。
- **結論句：**Such resistance is hurting the effectiveness of the policies, which may thus prolong the aging problem.
- **大意：**日本正在處理一個剛開始席捲全世界的問題，那就是人口老化與勞動力變少的問題。接著作者以問題解決法說明解決人口老化與勞動力變少的問題。

【問題解決法】常用字 / 片語：

solve, settle, clear up, straighten out, handle, take care of, deal with, tackle, tackle with, problem, solution, question, issue, trouble, difficulty。

十三、綜合法（Combined Methods, A Combination of Different Methods）

所謂綜合法，就是作者使用二種或二種以上的闡述或發展模式的方法。

A

Compulsive shopping often begins **at an early age**. Children who experienced parental neglect often grew up with low self-esteem **because** throughout much of their childhood they felt that they were not important as a person. **As a result**, they used toys to make up for their feelings of loneliness. **Because of** the ongoing sentiment of deprivation they endured as children, adults that have depended on materials for emotional support when they were much younger are more likely to become addicted to shopping. During adulthood, the purchase, instead of the toy, is substituted for affection. The victims are unable to deal with their everyday problems, especially those that alter their self-esteem. Important issues in their lives are repressed by buying something. **According to studies**, as many as **8.9 percent** of the American population qualify as compulsive buyers. Research has also found that men and women suffer from **this problem at about the same rate**.

Source：98 年大學指考

- **主題句：Compulsive shopping** often begins **at an early age**.
- **中心思想（關鍵字）：**compulsive shopping, at an early age。
- **闡述句策略：**綜合法（因果 because, As a result, because of）（舉例 According to, 8.9 percent）。
- **結論句：**Research has also found that men and women suffer from **this problem at about the same rate**.
- **大意：**強迫購買症常在早期就開始。接著作者說明強迫購買症的原因，同時引用研究資料顯示，美國人口中 8.9% 有此現象，且研究也發現，男士與女士遭受此問題的比率大約相同。

B

Learning style means a person's natural, habitual, and preferred way(s) of learning. Research about learning styles has identified gender differences. **For example**, one study found various differences between boys and girls in sensory learning styles. Girls were both more sensitive to sounds and more skillful at fine motor performance than boys. Boys, **in contrast**, showed an early visual superiority to girls. They were, however, clumsier than girls. They performed poorly at a detailed activity **such as** arranging a row of beads. **But** boys excelled at other activities that required total body coordination.

Source：93 年大學學測

- **主題句：**Learning style means a person's natural, habitual, and preferred way(s) of learning.
- **中心思想（關鍵字）：**learning styles。
- **闡述句策略：**綜合法（例證法 for example, such as）（對比法 in contrast, but）。

- **結論句：**N / A。
- **大意：**學習風格意謂一個人自然的、習慣性的，與較喜歡的學習方式。接著作者以例證法與對比法說明男孩與女孩學習風格的差異。

【第四章】

前言

許多學者主張：廣博閱讀（extensive reading）是增進學術能力的最佳途徑。中外的許多知名學者均持相同看法，例如聞名全球的雙語教育學者——美國南加大（University of Southern California, U.S.A）的 Professor Stephen Krashen、加拿大多倫多大學安大略教育研究所（Ontario Institute for Studies in Education, University of Toronto, Canada）的 Professor Jim Cummins，國內的中央大學柯華葳教授、洪蘭教授、李家同教授在其著作或文章中皆有類似的看法。

中外的國際實證研究亦支持了上述的主張。眾多的期刊文章已證實閱讀（譬如 FVR-free, voluntary reading）的效果遠超過以文法為核心的傳統教學，此類的研究大多以比較型研究（comparative study），即一組控制組（control group）（以文法為主的傳統教學）與一組實驗組（experimental group）（以閱讀為主的教學），經過一段時間的教學，兩組學生均參加標準化測試（standardized tests），資料顯示，不論是英語（文）的聽、說、讀、寫或文法的成效，實驗組學生的表現均優於控制組的學生。

編者教書時，發現閱讀成效的高低端視以下三個要素：一、字彙量，二、閱讀策略，三、廣博閱讀。首先，眾所周知，學生字彙量愈大時，愈容易理解原文段落或文章。增進字彙量有許多方法，而其中很有效的一個方法就是字源學的概念：即字根（word root / stem 字的意義）、字首（prefix 肯定 / 否定 / 方向 / 位置）、字尾（suffix 詞性：名詞 / 動詞 / 形容詞 / 副詞），若能熟悉字源學，可快速熟記英文單字。再者，閱讀策略方面，希望讀者能根據本書中所提及的方法，綜合運用 top-down reading strategy（由上而下閱讀策略）或 global strategy（總體的閱讀策略）與 bottom-up reading strategy（由下而上閱讀策略）或

local reading strategy（局部的閱讀策略）。最後，在廣博閱讀方面，讀者可以選擇較輕鬆的讀物，不用查單字，只要理解大意即可，因為悅讀（reading for pleasure, reading for fun）的效果最好。

本章著重學術文章段落的練習，並附上一些考題作為練習之用。

以下複習之前提過的文章三部曲與段落三部曲：

A.「文章三部曲」格式：IBC

Introduction（序論）、Body Paragraph(s)（本文）、Conclusion（結論）。

1. Introduction：文章的 thesis statement。
2. Body Paragraph(s)：每一段的 main / central idea。
3. Conclusion：複述文章的 thesis statement，改寫本文當中的 main / central idea(s)。

B.「段落三部曲」格式：TSC

Topic Sentence（主題句）、Supporting / Development Sentences（支持 / 發展句）、Concluding Sentence（結論句）。

1. Topic Sentence：main / central idea（中心思想或大意）。
2. Supporting / Development Sentences: supporting data, supporting evidence。
3. Concluding Sentence: repeat main / central idea。

句子大意與英文主、動詞練習

A

The birth (of cosmetic reconstructive surgery) truly occurred many hundreds of years later and over the past ten years plastic surgery has become very popular with more and more people refusing to grow old gracefully.

S. birth

V. occurred

Main idea: birth of cosmetic reconstructive surgery

【斷句練習】

1. 主詞 / 動詞 / 受詞（補語）一個單位間停頓。
2. 連接詞 / 對等連接詞之前停頓 and / or / but, either...or..., both...and..., neither...nor, not only...but also...。
3. 修飾語 / 介系詞之前停頓（of the..., who / which / that, p.p., Ving）。
4. 不定詞前停頓（to + V.）。
5. 片語前後停頓（e.g., in order to, along with, as well as, tackle with...）。
6. 平行結構前後停頓（e.g., through identifying, analyzing and responding to potential risks）。

解答

The birth / of cosmetic reconstructive surgery / truly occurred / many hundreds / of years later / and over the past ten years / plastic surgery / has become / very popular / with more and more people / refusing to grow old / gracefully.

B

The "image" of beauty (portrayed by the media) is usually related to the adjectives, young, very slim, and most often white.

S. image

V. is related to

Main idea: The image of beauty is usually related to the adjectives.

解答

The / “image” / of beauty / portrayed / by the media / is usually related / to the adjectives / , young / , very slim / , and most often white.

C

Sadly, for many people, the quest for beauty has turned into an all-out obsession.

S. quest

V. has turned into

Main idea: quest for beauty

解答

Sadly, / for many people, / the quest / for beauty / has turned / into an all-out obsession.

D

The first edition of Freud’s earliest writings on dreams was published in 1899.

S. edition

V. was published

Main idea: edition of Freud’s writing on dreams

解答

The first edition / of Freud’s earliest writings / on dreams / was published / in 1899.

E

All students who want to use the library borrowing services and the recreational, athletic, and entertainment facilities must have a valid summer identification card.

S. students

V. must have

Main idea: students must have a valid summer identification card

解答

All students / who want / to use / the library borrowing services / and the recreational / , athletic / , and entertainment facilities / must have / a valid summer identification card.

F

The rise in global temperature would also produce new patterns and extremes of drought and rainfall, seriously disrupting food production in certain regions.

S. rise

V. produce

Main idea: rise in global temperature, disrupting food production

解答

The rise / in global temperature / would also produce / new patterns / and extremes / of drought / and rainfall / , seriously disrupting / food production / in certain regions.

G

Extra greenhouse gases produced by man could cause a serious imbalance and push the Earth faster into a climactic disaster.

S. gases

V. cause, push

Main idea: Extra greenhouse gases could cause...and push....

解答

Extra greenhouse gases / produced / by man / could cause a serious imbalance / and push the Earth faster / into a climactic disaster.

H

Cancers that develop in the lymph nodes and blood are particularly dangerous since these are then spread throughout the rest of the body through the lymphatic system and circulatory system.

S. Cancers

V. are

Main idea: Cancers are particularly dangerous.

解答

Cancers / that develop / in the lymph nodes / and blood / are particularly dangerous / since these are then spread / throughout the rest / of the body / through the lymphatic system / and circulatory system.

I

Reports attacking the Bureau over two escapes by prisoners had been followed by the resignation of the former chief.

S. reports

V. had been followed

Main idea: Reports had been followed by the resignation of the former chief.

解答

Reports / attacking the Bureau / over two escapes / by prisoners / had been followed / by the resignation / of the former chief.

J

The taxonomies of common L2 reading strategies can be generally classified as either more "top-down" or more "bottom-up" in nature.

S. taxonomies

V. can be classified

Main idea: The taxonomies can be generally classified as either ... or ...

解答

The taxonomies / of common L2 reading strategies / can be generally classified as / either more "top-down" / or more "bottom-up" / in nature.

K

Compared with the abundant research into L2 paper-reading strategies, relatively few empirical studies have explored online reading strategies.

S. studies

V. have explored

Main idea: Few empirical studies have explored online reading strategies.

解答

Compared / with the abundant research / into L2 paper-reading strategies / , relatively few empirical studies / have explored / online reading strategies. （過去分詞構句，表被動）

Following the road, you will see the bus stop. （現在分詞構句，表主動）

Juding from (by) his appearance, he must be exhausted. （獨立分詞構句）

以上為分詞構句

常見的獨立分詞片語：Generally speaking... 一般來說……

Frankly speaking... 坦白說……

Judging from (by)... 由……判斷……

Considering... 考慮到……

Speaking of... 說到……

L

In comparing paper reading with hypermedia and multimedia reading strategies, Foltz (1993) found that readers used the same reading strategies in accessing these three (paper, hypermedia, and multimedia) types of texts.

S. Foltz

V. found

Main idea: readers used the same reading strategies

解答

In comparing paper reading / with hypermedia / and multimedia reading strategies / , Foltz (1993) / found / that / readers / used the same reading strategies / in accessing these three (paper / , hypermedia / , and multimedia) types / of texts.

M

All of these discoveries provide scientists with information both of the earth's history in general and on the area around the Grand Canyon in particular.

S. discoveries

V. provide...with...

Main idea: information

解答

All / of these discoveries / provide scientists / with information / both / of the earth's history / in general / and / on the area / around the Grand Canyon / in particular.

N

Those who have made thorough studies of the vocabularies of aboriginal languages have found that these languages have rich resources of available words.

S. those

V. have found

Main idea: these language have rich resources of available words

解答

Those / who have made / thorough studies / of the vocabularies / of aboriginal languages / have found / that / these languages / have rich resources / of available words.

P.S. 凡是……的人

Those (who V.) V.

People (who V.) V.

He who (who V-s / es) V.s / es

One who (who V-s / es) V.s / es

Restrictive vs. non-restrictive clause（限定與非限定子句用法）

1. My sister who lives in Canada will come back next week.
（我住在加拿大的姊姊下週會回來。）

說明：此句沒有逗號，為**限定**用法，表示說話者在加拿大的姊姊下週會回來，而說話者應該還有其他的姊姊。

2. My sister, who lives in Canada, will come back next week.
（我姊姊，她住在加拿大，下週會回來。）

說明：此句有逗號，為**非限定**用法，表示說話者只有一個姊姊，是獨一無二的，且下週會回來。

範例

English Sentences for Non-English Majors（非英語教學類）理工科

一、生醫類

1. Manipulation of single spins is essential for spin-based quantum information processing.

S. Manipulation

V. is

Main idea: manipulation

Source: *Neuroscience 2005 June 28*; 102(26): 9353-9358.

解答

Manipulation / of single spins / is essential / for spin-based quantum information processing.

2. The modern concept of neurogenesis in the adult brain is predicated on the premise that multipotent glial cells give rise to new neurons throughout life.

S. concept

V. is predicated

Main idea: conept of neurogenesis

Source: *Neuroscience 2005 June 28; 102*(26): 9353-9358.

解答

The modern concept / of neurogenesis / in the adult brain / is predicated / on the premise / that multipotent glial cells / give rise to / new neurons / throughout life.

3. Neurogenesis in the adult mammalian brain takes place in the subventricular zone (SVZ) of the lateral ventricular walls of the forebrain and in the subgranular layer of the dentate gyrus of the hippocampus.

S. neurogenesis

V. takes place

Main idea: neurogenesis takes place

Source: *Neuroscience 2005 June 28; 102*(26): 9353-9358.

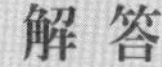
解答

Neurogenesis / in the adult mammalian brain / takes place / in the subventricular zone (SVZ) / of the lateral ventricular walls / of the forebrain / and / in the subgranular layer / of the dentate gyrus / of the hippocampus.

4. The results of the germination experiment (Fig. 2) suggest that the optimal time for running-water treatment is 2 days.

S. results

V. suggest

Main idea: results suggest

Source: *Neuroscience 2005 June 28; 102*(26): 9353-9358.

解答

The results / of the germination experiment (Fig. 2) / suggest / that the optimal time / for running-water treatment / is 2 days.

5. To investigate whether Shh could have a role in SVZ neurogenesis in the adult brain, we first analyzed the expression of Shh....

S. we

V. analyzed

Main idea. We analyzed the expression....

Source: *Neuroscience 2005 June 28; 102*(26): 9353-9358.

解 答

To investigate / whether Shh / could have a role / in SVZ neurogenesis / in the adult brain / , we first analyzed / the expression / of Shh....

6. The results presented here show that Archaea can constitute a constant and integral part of the activated sludge and that it can therefore beuseful to include Archaea in future studies of microbial communities in activated sludge.

S. results

V. show

Main idea: results show that...

Source: *Neuroscience 2005 June 28; 102*(26): 9353-9358.

解 答

The results / presented here / show / that Archaea / can constitute / a constant / and integral part / of the activated sludge / and that it / can therefore be useful / to include Archaea / in future studies / of microbial communities / in activated sludge.

二、電機類

1. Therefore, two-transistor power converters with soft-switching capabilities are normally considered, sometimes along with paralleling or interleaving arrangement.

S. (power) converters

V. are considered

Main idea: power converters are considered

Source: IEEE Transactions on Power Electronics, Vol. 26, No. 1, January 2011, 29-37.

解答

Therefore / , two-transistor power converters / with soft-switching capabilities / are normally considered / , sometimes along with / paralleling / or interleaving arrangement.

2. The active-clamp circuit recycles the energy stored in the magnetizing inductance of transformer to allow main / auxiliary switches turn-ON at zero-voltage switching and clamps the voltage stress of the main switches.

S. circuit

V. recycles

Main idea: circuit recycles the energy

Source: IEEE Transactions on Power Electronics, Vol. 26, No. 1, January 2011, 29-37.

解答

The active-clamp circuit / recycles the energy / stored / in the magnetizing inductance / of transformer / to allow main / auxiliary switches turn-ON / at zero-voltage switching / and clamps / the voltage stress / of the main switches.

3. More recently, LLC type of converter was reported in which soft switching can be achieved for the switches in both sides of the transformer, ZVS for the MOSFETs in the primary side and zero-current switching (ZCS) for the output diodes in the secondary side.

S. LLC type of converter

V. was reported

Main idea: LLC type of converter was reported

Source: IEEE Transactions on Power Electronics, Vol. 26, No. 1, January 2011, 29-37.

解答

More recently / , LLC type / of converter / was reported / in which soft switchin / can be achieved / for the switches / in both sides / of the transformer, ZVS / for the MOSFETs / in the primary side / and zero-current switching (ZCS) / for the output diodes / in the secondary side.

4. By keeping in mind the similarities of human hand shape with four fingers and one thumb, this paper aims to present a real time system for hand gesture recognition on the basis of detection of some meaningful shape based features like orientation, centre of mass (centroid), status of fingers, thumb in terms of raised or folded fingers of hand and their respective location in image.

S. this paper

V. aims

Main idea: This paper aims to present a real time system....

Source: IEEE Transactions on Power Electronics, Vol. 26, No. 1, January 2011, 29-37.

解答

By keeping in mind / the similarities / of human hand shap / e with four fingers / and one thumb / , this paper / aims / to present / a real time system / for hand gesture recognition / on the basis of / detection / of some meaningful shape based features / like orientation / , centre of mass (centroid) / , status of fingers / , thumb / in terms of raised / or folded fingers / of hand / and their respective location / in image.

三、機械類

1. Effect of brazing time on microstructure of the joints, as well as the dissolution behaviors of Cu interlayer was analyzed.

S. Effect

V. was analyzed

Main idea: Effect was analyzed.

Source: Trans. Nonferrous Met. Soc. China 21 (2011) 1035-1039.

解答

Effect / of brazing time / on microstructure / of the joints, as well as the dissolution behaviors / of Cu interlayer / was analyzed.

2. The base materials used in this study were commercial 6063 Al alloy and 1Cr18Ni9Ti stainless steel with dimensions of 15 mm×15 mm×2 mm.

S. materials

V. were

Main idea: materials were commercial 6063 A1 alloy and 1Cr18Ni9Ti stainless steel

Source: Trans. Nonferrous Met. Soc. China 21 (2011) 1035-1039.

解答

The base materials / used / in this study / were commercial 6063 Al alloy / and 1Cr18Ni9Ti stainless steel / with dimensions / of 15 mm×15 mm×2 mm.

3. In Fig.2, it seems that the whole reaction zone at the interface during contact reactive brazing includes the reactive layers near stainless steel side and the Al-Cu eutectic structure near Al side.

S. zone

V. includes

Main idea: zone includes the reactive layers

Source: Trans. Nonferrous Met. Soc. China 21 (2011) 1035-1039.

解答

In Fig.2 / , it seems that / the whole reaction zone / at the interface / during contact reactive brazing / includes the reactive layers / near stainless steel side / and the Al-Cu eutectic structure / near Al side.

4. To decide the suitable thickness of the interlayer and the contact reactive brazing parameters, we need to know the dissolution rate of Cu interlayer.

S. we

V. need

Main idea: We need to know the dissolution rate

Source: Trans. Nonferrous Met. Soc. China 21 (2011) 1035-1039.

解答

To decide / the suitable thickness / of the interlayer / and the contact reactive brazing parameters / , we need / to know / the dissolution rate / of Cu interlayer.

1. To further understand the relationship between the composition ratio and the mechanical properties, we need to do an analysis of the tensile fracture characteristics.

S. we

V. need

Main idea: We need to do an analysis....

Source: Materials and Design 39 (2012) 425-431.

解答

To further understand / the relationship / between the composition ratio / and the mechanical properties / , we need / to do an analysis / of the tensile fracture characteristics.

四、環安類

1. In order to study the distribution of temperature in different region, we used four Thermal Couple Clusters to measure the temperature of fire room and its adjoining room at different height.

S. we

V. used

Main idea: We used four Thermal Couple Clusters to....

Source: Procedia Engineering 11 (2011) 355-359.

解答

In order / to study the distribution / of temperature / in different region / , we used / four Thermal Couple Clusters / to measure / the temperature / of fire room / and its adjoining room / at different height.

2. A series of full scale fire tests with different fire locations in building, different fuel and different types of ceiling were conducted on wooden building.

S. fire tests

V. were conducted

Main idea: fire tests were conducted

Source: Procedia Engineering 11 (2011) 355-359.

解答

A series / of full scale fire tests / with different fire locations / in building, different fuel / and different types / of ceiling / were conducted / on wooden building.

1. Since Iijima discovered carbon nanotubes (CNTs) ark-discharge, their applications in various fields have been studied widely and intensely. CNTs have been the subject of much research interest in recent years owing to their attractive hysical, chemical, and material characteristics.

S. applications

V. have been studied

Main idea: applications have been studied

Source: Composites Science and Technology 68 (2008) 2954-2959.

解答

Since Iijima / discovered / carbon nanotubes (CNTs) ark-discharge / , their applications / in various fields / have been studied / widely / and intensely. CNTs / have been / the subject / of much research interest / in recent years / owing to their attractive physical / , chemical / , and material characteristics.

2. However, the literature on research on thermal analysis for CNTs has been slim.

S. literature

V. has been

Main idea: The literature has been slim.

Source: Composites Science and Technology 68 (2008) 2954-2959.

解答

However / , the literature / on research / on thermal analysis / for CNTs / has been slim.

3. The aim of this study was to explore the thermal and flammability properties of CCNT and to compare with the commercial CNT and powdered activated carbon in order to learn more about the possible applications of the material.

S. aim

V. was

Main idea: The aim was to explore....

Source: Composites Science and Technology 68 (2008) 2954-2959.

解答

The aim / of this study / was / to explore / the thermal / and flammability properties / of CCNT / and to compare / with the commercial CNT / and powdered activated carbon / in order to / learn more / about the possible applications / of the material.

五、營建工程類

1. Radio frequency identification (RFID) technology is an effective automated data collection technology that has been adopted by a number of industries.

S. RFID technology

V. is

Main idea: RFID technology is an....

Source: Journal of Construction Engineering and Management, Vol. 137, No. 12, December 1, 2011, 1089-1098.

解答

Radio frequency identification (RFID) technology / is an effective automated data collection technology / that has been adopted / by a number of / industries.

2. To provide a holistic examination of this implementation, we first present the state of the art of RFID technology and then demonstrate 39 academic research projects and construction industry use cases.

S. we

V. present, demonstrate

Main idea: We present and demonstrate

Source: Journal of Construction Engineering and Management, Vol. 137, No. 12, December 1, 2011, 1089-1098.

解答

To provide / a holistic examination / of this implementation / , we first present / the state of the art / of RFID technology / and then demonstrate / 39 academic research projects / and construction industry use cases.

1. During the lifecycle of construction projects, especially in the planning phase, the participants are confronted with enormous risk-based decision making (RBDM) problems, which are usually addressed through identifying, analyzing and responding to potential risks, and ultimately optimizing solutions.

S. participants

V. are confronted with

Main idea: The participants are confronted with enormous RBDM problems.

Source: Factors affecting contractors' risk attitudes in construction projects: Case study from China, *International Journal of Project Management 29* (2011) 209-219.

解答

During the lifecycle / of construction projects / , especially in the planning phase / , the participants / are confronted with / enormous risk-based decision making (RBDM) problems / , which are usually addressed / through identifying / , analyzing / and responding to potential risks / , and ultimately optimizing solutions.

2. The subjective judgment highly related to the human factors in the decision making process is customarily depicted as risk attitude, which plays an important role in decision making.

S. judgment

V. is depicted as

Main idea: The judgment is depicted as risk attitude.

Source: Factors affecting contractors' risk attitudes in construction projects: Case study from China, *International Journal of Project Management 29* (2011) 209-219.

解答

The subjective judgment / highly related to the human factors / in the decision making process / is customarily depicted / as risk attitude / , which plays an important role / in decision making.

3. Most previous studies in construction project risk management have been focusing on the factors contributing to the success of risk management, but little attention was given to factors significantly affecting decision makers' risk attitudes in construction projects.

S. studies

V. have been focusing on

Main idea: Most previous studies have been focusing on the factors....

Source: Factors affecting contractors' risk attitudes in construction projects: Case study from China, *International Journal of Project Management 29* (2011) 209-219.

解答

Most previous studies / in construction project risk management / have been focusing / on the factors / contributing to the success / of risk management / , but little attention / was given / to factors / significantly affecting decision makers' risk attitudes / in construction projects.

六、企管類

1. The point of departure for this paper is a number of contingency-theory studies on the relationship between business strategy and the design and use of management control.

S. point

V. is

Main idea: point of departure is

Source: British Journal of Management Vol. 11, 197-212 (2000).

解答

The point / of departure / for this paper / is a number of / contingency-theory studies / on the relationship / between business strategy / and the design / and use / of management control.

2. Unlike most previous studies in the filed, this paper discusses how the strategic variables taken together may be assumed to influence the classification of strategy and thus the design and use of the management-control system.

S. this paper

V. discusses

Main idea: This paper discusses how....

Source: British Journal of Management Vol. 11, 197-212 (2000).

解答

Unlike most previous studies / in the filed / , this paper / discusses / how the strategic variables / taken together / may be assumed / to influence / the classification / of strategy / and thus the design / and use / of the management-control system.

3. Our deductive analysis, and the hypotheses used in connection with it, show that studies which consider only one strategic variable may lead to erroneous conclusions about the relationship strategy and management control.

S. analysis and hypotheses

V. show

Main idea: analysis and hypotheses show that....

Source: British Journal of Management Vol. 11, 197-212 (2000).

解答

Our deductive analysis / , and the hypotheses / used / in connection with it / , show that studies / which consider only one strategic variable / may lead to erroneous conclusions / about the relationship / between strategy / and management control.

4. Interest in the research area of strategy and management control has increased significantly in recent years.

S. interest

V. has increased

Main idea: interest has increased

Source: British Journal of Management Vol. 11, 197-212 (2000).

解答

Interest / in the research area / of strategy / and management control / has increased / significantly / in recent years.

5. One indication of this growing interest is the impact of methods like the balanced scorecard, strategic management accounting, and value-based management.

S. indication

V. is

Main idea: indication is

Source: British Journal of Management Vol. 11, 197-212 (2000).

解答

One indication / of this growing interest / is the impact / of methods / like the balanced scorecard / , strategic management accounting / , and value-based management.

6. Moreover, with the growth of interest in the zone where strategy and management control intermesh, there has been a renewed interest in many of the business-strategy typologies, which were proposed in the 1970s and 1980s.

S. there

V. has been

Main idea: there has been a renewed interest in....

Source: British Journal of Management Vol. 11, 197-212 (2000).

解答

Moreover / , with the growth / of interest / in the zone / where strategy / and management control intermesh / , there has been / a renewed interest / in many / of the business-strategy typologies / , which were proposed / in the 1970s / and 1980s.

七、資工類

1. Cache contention for shared resources on multicore remains an unsolved problem in existing systems despite significant research efforts dedicated to this problem in the past.

S. cache contention

V. remains

Main idea: cache contention remains an unsolved problem

Source: Addressing Shared Resource Contention in Multicore Processors via Scheduling.

解答

Cache contention / for shared resources / on multicore / remains / an unsolved problem / in existing systems / despite significant research efforts / dedicated to this problem / in the past.

2. The most difficult part of the problem is to find a classification scheme for threads, which would determine how they affect each other when competing for shared resources.

S. part

V. is

Main idea: The part is to find a classification scheme for....

Source: Addressing Shared Resource Contention in Multicore Processors via Scheduling.

解答

The most difficult part / of the problem / is to find a classification scheme / for threads, which would determine / how they affect each other / when competing / for shared resources.

3. Through extensive experimentation on real systems as opposed to simulators, we determined that cache contention is not the dominant cause of performance degradation of threads co-scheduled to the same last-level cache (LLC).

S. we

V. determined

Main idea: We determined that cache contention is not the dominant cause....

Source: Addressing Shared Resource Contention in Multicore Processors via Scheduling.

解答

Through extensive experimentation / on real systems / as opposed to simulators / , we determined / that / cache contention / is not the dominant cause / of performance degradation / of threads / co-scheduled / to the same last-level cache (LLC).

4. Along with cache contention, other factors like memory controller contention, memory bus contention, and prefetching hardware contention all combine in complex ways to create the performance degradation that threads experience when sharing an LLC.

S. factors

V. combine

Main idea: other factors all combine to create the performance degradation....

Source: Addressing Shared Resource Contention in Multicore Processors via Scheduling.

解答

Along with cache contention / , other factors / like memory controller contention / , memory bus contention / , and prefetching hardware contention / all combine / in complex ways / to create / the performance degradation / that threads experience / when sharing an LLC.

1. Although Transmission Control Protocol (TCP) works well in wired networks, it fails to offer satisfactory performance in lossy and wireless environments.

S. it

V. fails

Main idea: It fails to offer satisfactory performance....

Source: Engineering TCP transmission and retransmission mechanisms for wireless networks.

解答

Although Transmission Control Protocol (TCP) / works well / in wired networks / , it fails / to offer / satisfactory performance / in lossy / and wireless environments.

2. The selective acknowledgment (SACK) header option is commonly considered the best choice for end-to-end traffic control in wireless networks.

S. SACK header option

V. is

Main idea: SACK header option is considered the best choice....

Source: Engineering TCP transmission and retransmission mechanisms for wireless networks.

解答

The selective acknowledgment (SACK) header option / is commonly considered / the best choice / for end-to-end traffic control / in wireless networks.

3. Being designed as an option, any flow control family can use this option to improve the system's performance, if needed.

S. flow control family

V. can use

Main idea: Any flow control family can use this option to....

Source: Engineering TCP transmission and retransmission mechanisms for wireless networks.

解答

Being designed / as an option / , any flow control family / can use / this option / to improve / the system's performance / , if needed.

段落練習

範例1

It took me a long while to realize that there was something more for me to learn about beauty. Beauty standards vary with culture. In Samoa a woman is not considered attractive unless she weighs more than 200 pounds. More importantly, if it's happiness that we want, why not put our energy there rather than on the size of our body? Why not look inside? Many of us strive hard to change our body, but in vain. We have to find a way to live comfortably inside our body and make friends with and cherish ourselves. When we change our attitudes toward ourselves, the whole world changes.

Source：94 年大學學測

- **主題句：**It took me a long while to realize that there was something more for me to learn about beauty.
- **中心思想（關鍵字）：**beauty。
- **發展句策略：**例證法（In Somoa a woman is not considered attractive ....）。
- **結論句：**When we change our attitudes toward ourselves, the whole world changes.
- **大意：**我花很久的時間才了解到「美」的涵意。接著作者以例證法——薩摩亞（西南太平洋一個群島）的女士為例說明。

範例2

The mind and body work together to produce stress, which is a bodily response to a stimulus, a response that disturbs the body's normal physiological balance. However, stress is not always bad. For example, a stress reaction can sometimes save a person's life by releasing hormones that enable a person to react quickly and with greater energy in a dangerous situation. In everyday situations, too, stress can provide that extra push needed to do something difficult. But too much stress often injures both the mind and the body. How can stress be kept under control? *Learn to Lighten Up and Live Longer*, the best seller of the month, has several good suggestions. So, grab a copy and start learning how you can reduce stress in your life.

Source：95 年大學學測

- **主題句：**However, stress is not always bad.
- **中心思想（關鍵字）：**stress。
- **發展句策略：**例證法（For example）。
- **結論句：**So, grab a copy and start learning how you can reduce stress in your life.
- **大意：**壓力不一定是壞事。接著作者以例證法說明壓力反應有時候可以拯救一個人的性命，因為人遇到危險情況時，藉著釋放荷爾蒙，可以用較大能源迅速反應。

範例3

The first high school proms were held in the 1920s in America. By the 1930s, proms were common across the country. For many older Americans, the prom was a modest, home-grown affair in the school gymnasium. Prom-goers were well dressed but not fancily dressed up for the occasion: boys wore jackets and ties and girls their Sunday dresses. Couples danced to music provided by a local amateur band or a record player. After the 1960s, and especially since the 1980s, the high school prom in many areas has become a serious exercise in excessive consumption, with boys renting expensive tuxedos and girls wearing designer gowns. Stretch limousines were hired to drive the prom-goers to expensive restaurants or discos for an all-night extravaganza.

Source：99 年大學學測

- **主題句：**The first high school proms were held in the 1920s in America.
- **中心思想（關鍵字）：**first high school proms。
- **發展句策略：**時間順序法（**1920s, 1930s, 1960s, 1980s**）。
- **結論句：**Stretch limousines were hired to drive the prom-goers to expensive restaurants or discos for an all-night extravaganza.
- **大意：**第一個高中音樂會於美國 1920 年代首度舉辦。接著作者以時間順序法說明高中音樂會於美國發展的經過。

範例4

Many visitors to Italy avoid its famous cities, preferring instead the quiet countryside of Tuscany, located in the rural heart of the country. Like the rest of Italy, Tuscany has its share of art and architectures, because travelers are drawn more by its gentle hills, by its country estates, and by its hilltop villages. This is not an area to rush through but to enjoy slowly, like a glass of fine wine produced here. Many farmhouses offer simple yet comfortable accommodations. From such a base, the visitors can explore the nearby towns and countryside, soak up the sunshine, or just relax in the company of a good book.

Source：101 年專門職業及技術人員普通考試導遊人員、領隊人員考試試題

- **主題句：**Many visitors to Italy avoid its famous cities, preferring instead the quiet countryside of Tuscany, located in the rural heart of the country.
- **中心思想（關鍵字）：**quiet countryside of Tuscany。
- **發展句策略：**空間法（located, nearby）。
- **結論句：**From such a base, the visitors can explore the nearby towns and countryside, soak up the sunshine, or just relax in the company of a good book.
- **大意：**許多到義大利的觀光客避免去有名的都市，反而較喜歡去安靜的 Tuscany 鄉下。

範例5

If a historian is investigating causes for the decline of the Roman Empire, should he learn the moment when the Great Wall of China was built? Is this a relevant fact? On further investigation we find that it is. There does appear to be a cause-and-effect relationship between the building of the Chinese Wall and the decline of the Roman Empire. The Chinese build the Great Wall to protect their borders. After the Wall was built, the Huns advanced on China but was stopped by the wall. Unable to move east, they turned westward and finally reached Roman territory. There they contributed significantly to the fall of the Roman Empire.

Source：99 學年度臺大碩士班招生考試

- **主題句：**If a historian is investigating causes for the decline of the Roman Empire, should he learn the moment when the Great Wall of China was built?

- **中心思想（關鍵字）：**causes。
- **闡述句策略：**因果法（cause-and-effect relationship）。
- **結論句：**There they contributed significantly to the fall of the Roman Empire.
- **大意：**羅馬帝國衰落與中國長城之間有因果關係。

範例6

Fans of professional baseball and football argue continually over which is America's favorite sport. Though the figures on attendance for each vary with every new season, certain arguments remain the same. To begin with, football is a quicker, more physical sport, and football fans enjoy the emotional involvement they feel while watching. Baseball, on the other hand, seems more mental, like chess, and attracts those fans that prefer a quieter, more complicated game.In addition, professional football teams usually play no more than fourteen games a year. Baseball teams, however, play almost every day for six months. Finally, football fans seem to love the half-time activities, the marching bands, and the pretty cheerleaders. On the contrary, baseball fans are more content to concentrate on the game's finer details and spend the breaks between innings filling out their own private scorecards.

Source：95 年大學學測

- **主題句：**Fans of professional baseball and football argue continually over which is America's favorite sport.
- **中心思想（關鍵字）：**America's favorite sport。

- **發展句策略：**對比法（Baseball, on the other hand, On the contrary）。
- **結論句：**N / A。
- **大意：**職業棒球與橄欖球的粉絲們繼續不斷地爭論，議論那一個才是美國人最喜歡的運動。接著作者以對比法對比職業棒球與橄欖球的各種相異處。

範例7

Do women really use language differently from men? Over the years, researchers have given different answers to this question. In the legends of some cultures, it is even claimed that men and women speak different languages. If this were true, how could boys communicate with their mothers? One research report shows men and women use much the same grammar and vocabulary in English, although each sex uses certain kinds of words and structures more frequently than the other. Most men use more swear words, while far more women use adjectives such as "super" and "lovely," and exclamations such as "Goodness me!" and "Oh dear!" Women have been found to ask more questions, make more use of positive and encouraging "noises," use a wider range of intonation patterns, and make greater use of the pronouns "you" and "we." By contrast, men are much more likely to interrupt (about three times as often in some studies), to argue about what has been said, to ignore or respond poorly to what has been said, to introduce more new topics into the conversation, and to make more assertions.

Source：91 年大學學測

- **主題句：**Do women really use language differently from men?
- **中心思想（關鍵字）：**use language differently。
- **發展句策略：**對比法（By contrast）。
- **結論句：**N / A。
- **大意：**女士與男士使用語言有所不同嗎？接著作者以對比法對比女士與男士使用語言之不同處。

範例8

Onions can be divided into two categories: fresh onions and storage onions. Fresh onions are available in yellow, red and white throughout their season, March through August. They can be identified by their thin, light-colored skin. Because they have a higher water content, they are typically sweeter and milder tasting than storage onions. This higher water content also makes it easier for them to bruise. With its delicate taste, the fresh onion is an ideal choice for salads and other lightly-cooked dishes. Storage onions, on the other hand, are available August through April. Unlike fresh onions, they have multiple layers of thick, dark, papery skin. They also have an intense flavor and a higher percentage of solids. For these reasons, storage onions are the best choice for spicy dishes that require longer cooking times or more flavor.

Source：99 年大學學測

- **主題句：**Onions can be divided into two categories: fresh onions and storage onions.
- **中心思想（關鍵字）：**two categories。

- **發展句策略：**分類法（fresh onions, storage onions）。
- **結論句：**N / A。
- **大意：**洋蔥分成二種：新鮮的洋蔥與儲藏的洋蔥。接著作者以分類法說明新鮮的洋蔥與儲藏的洋蔥。

範例9

There are three kinds of tea: black, green, and oolong. Most international tea trading is in black tea. Black tea preparation consists mainly of picking young leaves and leaf buds on a clear sunny day and letting the leaves dry for about an hour in the sun. Then, they are lightly rolled and left in a fermentation room to develop scent and a red color. Next, they are heated several more times. Finally, the leaves are dried in a basket over a charcoal fire. Green tea leaves are heated in steam, rolled, and dried. Oolong tea is prepared similarly to black tea, but without the fermentation time.

Source：95 年大學學測

- **主題句：**There are three kinds of tea: black, green, and oolong.
- **中心思想（關鍵字）：**three kinds。
- **發展句策略：**分類法（black, green, and oolong）。
- **結論句：**N / A。
- **大意：**茶分成三種：紅茶、綠茶與烏龍茶。接著作者以分類法依序介紹此三種茶。
- **註：**紅茶為全發酵茶，烏龍茶為半發酵茶，綠茶為未發酵茶（兒茶素較多）。胃較好者可飲用綠茶；反之，胃較不好者可飲用紅茶。烏龍茶則屬中庸之茶。

範例10

Children's encounters with poetry should include three types of response-enjoyment, exploration, and deepening understanding. These do not occur always as separate steps but may happen simultaneously. Certainly, children must start with enjoyment or their interest in poetry dies. But if from the beginning they find delight in the poems they hear or read, they are ready and eager to explore further-more books and more poems of different sorts. Even the youngest children can learn to see implications beyond the obvious. To read for hidden meanings is to identify with the poet, to ask the poet's questions. This is reading for deeper understanding, taking a thoughtful look at what lies beneath the surface. Enjoyment, exploration, and deeper understanding must all be part of children's experience with poetry if we are to help them to love it.

Source：93 年大學指考

- **主題句：**Children's encounters with poetry should include three types of response-enjoyment, exploration, and deepening understanding.
- **中心思想（關鍵字）：**three types of response。
- **發展句策略：**分類法（enjoyment, exploration, deepening understanding）。
- **結論句：**Enjoyment, exploration, and deeper understanding must all be part of children's experience with poetry if we are to help them to love it.
- **大意：**孩子們與詩接觸時，應該包含三種反應——樂趣、探索與加深的領會。接著作者以分類法依序說明此三種反應。

範例11

The term "standard of living" usually refers to the economic well-being enjoyed by a person, family, community, or nation. A standard of living is considered high when it includes not only necessities but also certain comforts and luxuries; it is considered low when food, clean water, housing, and other necessities are limited or lacking.

Source：92年大學學測

- **主題句：**The term "standard of living" usually refers to the economic well-being enjoyed by a person, family, community, or nation.
- **中心思想（關鍵字）：**standard of living。
- **闡述句策略：**定義法（refers to）。
- **結論句：**N / A。
- **大意：**生活水準這個名詞通常指一個人、家庭、社區或國家享有的經濟福利。接著作者以定義法說明生活水準高低的定義。

範例12

Experts say that creativity by definition means going against the tradition and breaking the rules. To be creative, you must dare to rebel, and courageously express your own outlook and take pride in what makes you unique. But does our society encourage children to break the rules? I'm afraid the answer is no. The famous film director Ang Lee recalls his father's disappointment with him when he was young. As a small child, he would pick up a broom and pretend to be playing guitar for the entertainment of family guests. Then, when he was studying film in college, he would exhaust himself just for a performance tour. His father, who always hoped that he would get a PhD and become a professor, reacted with a scoff: "What is all this nonsense?!" But it later turned out that it was exactly his courage to "rebel" and to express his own ideas that marks his films with distinct creativity.

Source：94 年大學學測

- **主題句：**Experts say that creativity by definition means going against the tradition and breaking the rules.
- **中心思想（關鍵字）：**creativity。
- **闡述句策略：**定義法（by definition, means）。
- **結論句：**But it later turned out that it was exactly his courage to "rebel" and to express his own ideas that marks his films with distinct creativity.
- **大意：**專家說創意以定義上來說，就是反對傳統與打破規則。接著作者以定義法說明創意的定義，並以著名導演李安為例說明創意的意義。

範例13

Now that you are planning to go to college, **how** can you **select** an ideal college for yourself? By its reputation or the test scores it requires for admission? In fact, it is not as simple as that. College education is far more complicated than just the reputation of a college or the test scores it requires. In addition to these two factors, you should also have other important information. Finding out which college suits you involves time and energy, but no more than those you might spend on buying a motorcycle or a computer.

Here are some **tips** on choosing an ideal one from a number of colleges.

1. Visit the websites of these colleges and find out which college has departments offering courses that interest you or will help you prepare for your future career.
2. Are the professors in the departments you plan to get into experts in their own fields?
3. Do the colleges allow you to participate in activities that will help you develop yourself intellectually and emotionally?

I hope the above advice is helpful to you in selecting the right college.

Source：91 年大學學測

- **主題句：**Now that you are planning to go to college, how can you select an ideal college for yourself ?
- **中心思想（關鍵字）：**how, select。
- **闡述句策略：**問題解決法（tips）。
- **結論句：**I hope the above advice is helpful to you in selecting the right college.
- **大意：**既然你正計畫要上大學，你如何為你自己選擇一個理想的大學？接著作者提供一些選擇理想大學的提示（或建議）。

文章練習

範例1

A sense of humor is something highly valued. A person who has a great sense of humor is often considered to be happy and socially confident. However, humor is a double-edged sword. It can forge better relationships and help you cope with life, but sometimes it can also damage self-esteem and antagonize others.

People who use bonding humor tell jokes and generally lighten the mood. They're perceived as being good at reducing the tension in uncomfortable situations. They often make fun of their common experiences, and sometimes they may even laugh off their own misfortunes. The basic message they deliver is: We're all alike, we find the same things funny, and we're all in this together.

Put-down humor, on the other hand, is an aggressive type of humor used to criticize and manipulate others through teasing. When it's aimed against politicians, as it often is, it's hilarious and mostly harmless. But in the real world, it may have a harmful impact. An example of such humor is telling friends an embarrassing story about another friend. When challenged about their teasing, the put-down jokers might claim that they are "just kidding," thus allowing themselves to avoid responsibility. This type of humor, though considered by some people to be socially acceptable, may hurt the feelings of the one being teased and thus take a toll on personal relationships.

Finally, in hate-me humor, the joker is the target of the joke for the amusement of others. This type of humor was used by comedians John Belushi and Chris Farley-both of whom suffered for their success in show business. A small dose of such humor is charming, but routinely offering oneself up to be humiliated erodes one's self-respect, and fosters depression and anxiety.

So it seems that being funny isn't necessarily an indicator of good social skills and well-being. In certain cases, it may actually have a negative impact on interpersonal relationships.

Source：101 年大學指考

- **Introduction（引言段）：**

Thesis Statement：However, humor is a double-edged sword.（然而，幽默是一把雙刃的劍）。

- **第二段：**

主題句：People who use bonding humor tell jokes and generally lighten the mood.

中心思想（關鍵字）：bonding humor。

闡述句策略：中間掃描描述法（They're perceived as....)。

結論句：The basic message they deliver is: We're all alike, we find the same things funny, and we're all in this together.

- **第三段：**

主題句：Put-down humor, on the other hand, is an aggressive type of humor used to criticize and manipulate others through teasing.

中心思想（關鍵字）：put-down humor。

闡述句策略：中間掃描例證法（An example of such humor is....)。

結論句：This type of humor, though considered by some people to be socially acceptable, may hurt the feelings of the one being teased and thus take a toll on personal relationships.

- **第四段：**

主題句：Finally, in hate-me humor, the joker is the target of the joke for the amusement of others.

中心思想（關鍵字）：hate-me humor。

闡述句策略：中間掃描例證法（comedians John Belushi and Chris Farley）。

結論句：A small dose of such humor is charming, but routinely offering oneself up to be humiliated erodes one's self-respect, and fosters depression and anxiety.

- **Conclusion（結論段）：**

Thesis statement：So it seems that being funny isn't necessarily an indicator of good social skills and well-being.（所以有趣並不一定是擁有良好社交技巧與康樂的指標）。

範例2

Although stories about aliens have never been officially confirmed, their existence has been widely speculated upon.

Many people believe that beings from outer space have visited us for centuries. Some say that life on Earth originated "out there" and was seeded here. Others say that aliens have kept an eye on what happens on Earth, and are responsible for quite a few legends, and that the ancient Greek and Roman gods, as well as the fairies and dwarfs in many classical tales, were in fact "space people" living here.

Still others say that aliens were responsible for the growth of highly evolved civilizations which have since perished, including the Incan and Mayan civilizations and the legendary Atlantis.

A lot of ancient civilizations, like the Egyptians, Hindus, Greeks, and Mayans, have left writings and drawings which indicate contacts with superior beings "from the stars." Many believe that the aliens are here to help us, while others hold that the aliens intend us harm. Still others think that most aliens visit Earth to study us like our scientists study primitive natives and animals, and have no interest in helping us in any way.

It is difficult to comment conclusively on these theories in general, apart from saying that any and all of them might be possible. Maybe time will tell.

Source：93 年大學學測

- **Introduction（引言段）：**

Thesis Statement：Although stories about aliens have never been officially confirmed, their existence has been widely speculated upon.（雖然有關外星人的故事從未被官方證實，然而人們一直廣泛地推測他們的存在）。

- **第二段：**

主題句：Many people believe that beings from outer space have visited us for centuries.

中心思想（關鍵字）：beings。

闡述句策略：中間掃描例證法（Some, Others, Still others）。

結論句：N / A。

- **第三段：**

主題句： A lot of ancient civilizations, like the Egyptians, Hindus, Greeks, and Mayans, have left writings and drawings which indicate contacts with superior beings "from the stars."

中心思想（關鍵字）： ancient civilizations。

闡述句策略： 中間掃描例證法（Many, Others, Still others）。

結論句： N / A。

- **Conclusioin（結論段）：**

Thesis statement： Maybe time will tell.（也許時間會說明一切）。

範例3

All advertising includes an attempt to persuade. To put it another way, ads are communication designed to get someone to do something. Even if an advertisement claims to be purely informational, it still has persuasion at its core. The ad informs the consumers with one purpose: to get the consumer to like the brand and, on that basis, to eventually buy the brand. Without this persuasive intent, communication about a product might be news, but it would not be advertising.

Advertising can be persuasive communication not only about a product but also an idea or a person. Political advertising is one example. Although political ads are supposed to be concerned with the public welfare, they are paid for and they all have a persuasive intent. They differ from commercial ads in that political ads "sell" candidates rather than commercial goods. A Bush campaign ad, for instance, did not ask anyone to buy anything, yet it attempted to persuade American citizens to view George Bush favorably. Aside from campaign advertising, political advertising is also used to persuade people to support or oppose proposals. Critics of President Clinton's health care plan used advertising to influence lawmakers and defeat the government's plan.

In addition to political parties, environmental groups and human rights organizations also buy advertising to persuade people to accept their way of thinking. For instance, the international organization Greenpeace uses advertising to get their message out. In the ads, they warn people about serious pollution problems and the urgency of protecting the environment. They, too, are selling something and trying to make a point.

Source：101 年大學指考

- **Introduction（引言段）：**

Thesis Statement： All advertising includes an attempt to persuade.（所有的廣告都包括嘗試說服別人）。

- **第二段：**

主題句： Advertising can be persuasive communication not only about a product but also an idea or a person.

中心思想（關鍵字）： not only about a product but also an idea or a person。

闡述句策略： 中間掃描例證法（for instance）。

結論句： N / A。

- **第三段：**

主題句： In addition to political parties, environmental groups and human rights organizations also buy advertising to persuade people to accept their way of thinking.

中心思想（關鍵字）：environmental groups and human rights organizations。

闡述句策略：中間掃描例證法（For instance,）。

結論句：They, too, are selling something and trying to make a point.

- **Conclusion（結論段）：**

本文無結論段。

範例4

In all cultures and throughout history hair has had a special significance. In ancient Egypt, as long ago as 1500 BC, the outward appearance expressed the person's status, role in society and political position. Wigs played an important role in this: they were crafted with great artistry and often sprinkled with powdered gold.

In the 8th century BC, the pre-Roman Celts in Northern Europe wore their hair long. In a man it was the expression of his strength, in a woman of her fertility. The idea of long hair as a symbol of male strength is even mentioned in the Bible, in the story of Samson and Delilah. Samson was a leader of the Israelites. His long hair, which he never cut, gave him superhuman powers. The only person who knew his secret was Delilah. However, she spied for the enemy and betrayed him. One night she cut off his hair and thus robbed him of his strength.

In the classical Greek period, curly hair was not only the fashion, but it also represented an attitude towards life. Curls or locks were the metaphor for change, freedom and the joy of living. The ancient Greek word for curls and locks is related to intriguing and tempting someone.

Hair is also used as a symbol of opposition. The punk protest movement today uses hair as a symbol of disapproval of the "middle-class, conventional lifestyle" by wearing provocative haircuts and shockingly colored hair. A different form of objection could be seen in the women's hairstyles in the 1960s. Women's liberation was expressed in a short-cut, straight and simple hairstyle which underlined equality with men without neglecting female attributes. To this day hair has kept its importance as a symbol of power, youth, vitality and health.

Source：98 年大學指考

- **Introduction（引言段）：**

Thesis Statement：In all cultures and throughout history hair has had a special significance.（在所有的文化中與歷史上，頭髮曾經有過特殊的重要性）。

- **第二段：**

主題句：In the 8th century BC, the pre-Roman Celts in Northern Europe wore their hair long.

中心思想（關鍵字）：long hair。

闡述句策略：中間掃描對比法（man vs. woman）、例證法（Bible）。

結論句：N / A。

- **第三段：**

主題句：In the classical Greek period, curly hair was not only the fashion, but it also represented an attitude towards life.

中心思想（關鍵字）：an attitude towards lilfe。

闡述句策略：中間掃描例證法（metaphor for change, freedom and the joy of living）。

結論句：N / A。

- **Conclusion（結論段）：**

Thesis statement：To this day hair has kept its importance as a symbol of power, youth, vitality and health.（時至今日，頭髮都保持其重要性，它是權力、青春、活力與健康的象徵）。

範例5

The best-known technological aid in language teaching is undoubtedly the language laboratory－a room, usually divided into booths, where students can listen individually to tape recordings of foreign language material, and where they may record and play back their own responses, while being monitored by a teacher.

When these laboratories were first introduced, they were heralded as a technique that would improve the rate and quality of language learning. They would take the burden of repetitive drills away from the teacher, provide more opportunities for learners to practice listening and speaking, and enable them to develop at their own rates and monitor their own progress. Many schools were quick to install expensive laboratory equipment. However, within a few years, it became apparent that there would be no breakthrough. The **expected improvements** did not materialize, and the popularity of the "language lab" showed a marked decline.

There were several reasons for the language lab's failure to live up to expectations. The taped materials were often poorly designed, leading to student frustration and boredom. The published programs failed to reflect the kind of work the student was doing in class. Few modern languages staff had received training in materials design or laboratory use. And it proved difficult to maintain the equipment once it had been installed.

Today, the strengths and limitations of the laboratory are better realized, and the vastly increased potential of modern electronic hardware has led to a certain revival. There is now considerable interest in *language learning laboratories*, which contain much more than the traditional systems-in particular, the introduction of interactive computational aids and video materials has proved to be extremely popular.

It is now clear that, when used properly, laboratories can provide a valuable extra dimension to language teaching. For example, the taped material can provide a variety of authentic and well-recorded models for the training of listening comprehension. And laboratories can be used as resource centers, or libraries, giving learners extra opportunities to practice at their chosen level.

Source：93 年大學學測

- **Introduction（引言段）：**

Thesis Statement： The best-known technological aid in language teaching is undoubtedly the language laboratory.（語言教學中最有名的科技上的教具，無疑的就是語言實驗室）。

- **第二段：**

主題句： When these laboratories were first introduced, they were heralded as a technique that would improve the rate and quality of language learning.

中心思想（關鍵字）： technique。

闡述句策略： 中間掃描描述法（They would take the burden....）。

結論句： N / A。

- **第三段：**

主題句： There were several reasons for the language lab's failure to live up to expectations.

中心思想（關鍵字）： several reasons。

闡述句策略： 中間掃描例證法（taped materials, published programs）。

結論句： And it proved difficult to maintain the equipment once it had been installed.

- **第四段：**

主題句： Today, the strengths and limitations of the laboratory are better realized, and the vastly increased potential of modern electronic hardware has led to a certain revival.

中心思想（關鍵字）： revival。

闡述句策略： 中間掃描例證法（language learning laboratories）。

結論句： N / A。

- **Conclusion（結論段）：**

Thesis statement： It is now clear that, when used properly, laboratories can provide a valuable extra dimension to language teaching.（很清楚的，當我們妥善使用時，語言實驗室對於語言教學可以提供很有價值的另一特點）。

範例6

Andrew Carnegie, once the world's richest person, was born in 1835 to a weaver's family in Scotland. As a child, he was expected to follow his father's profession. But the industrial revolution destroyed the weavers' craft, and the family had to leave for new possibilities in America.

In 1848 the Carnegies arrived in Pittsburgh, then the iron-manufacturing center of the country. Young Carnegie took odd jobs at a cotton factory and later worked as a messenger boy in the telegraph office. He was often asked to deliver messages to the city theater, where he would stay to watch plays by great playwrights. He also spent most of his leisure hours in a small library that a local benefactor made available to working boys.

After the Civil War, Carnegie saw great potential in the iron industry. He devoted himself to the replacement of wooden bridges with stronger iron ones and earned a fortune. He further introduced a new steel refining process to convert iron into steel. By 1900, Carnegie Steel produced more of the metal than all of Great Britain.

However, Carnegie often expressed his uneasiness with the businessman's life. Wishing to spend more time receiving instruction and reading systematically, he once wrote, "To continue much longer overwhelmed by business cares and with most of my thoughts wholly upon the way to make more money in the shortest time, must degrade me beyond hope of permanent recovery." The strong desire for intellectual pursuit led him to sell his company and retire at 64.

Fond of saying that "the man who dies rich dies disgraced," Carnegie then turned his attention to giving away his fortune. He abhorred charity; instead, he used his money to help others help themselves. He established over 2,500 public libraries, and sponsored numerous cultural, educational and scientific institutions. By the time he died in 1919, he had given away 350 million dollars.

Source：92 年大學指考

- **Introduction（引言段）：**

Thesis Statement：But the industrial revolution destroyed the weavers' craft, and the family had to leave for new possibilities in America.（但是工業革命破壞了織布工的行業，所以這家人必須前往美國尋找新的機會）。

- **第二段：**

主題句：In 1848 the Carnegies arrived in Pittsburgh, then the iron-manufacturing center of the country.

中心思想（關鍵字）：iron-manufactruing center of the country。

闡述句策略：中間掃描描述法（Young Carnegie took odd jobs....）。

結論句：N / A。

- **第三段：**

主題句：After the Civil War, Carnegie saw great potential in the iron industry.

中心思想（關鍵字）：great potential。

闡述句策略：中間掃描描述法（He devoted himself to the ....）。

結論句：By 1900, Carnegie Steel produced more of the metal than all of Great Britain.

第四段：

主題句：However, Carnegie often expressed his uneasiness with the businessman's life.

中心思想（關鍵字）：uneasiness。

闡述句策略：中間掃描描述法（Wishing to spend more time....）。

結論句：The strong desire for intellectual pursuit led him to sell his company and retire at 64.

Conclusion（結論段）：

Thesis statement：Carnegie then turned his attention to giving away his fortune.（然後卡內基將他的注意力轉移到贈送分發他的財富）。

大學學測英文閱讀測驗

應付考題時，閱讀策略是：

(1) 先看考題，再看文章。

(2) 看整篇文章的 organizational pattern（組織方式）。

(3) 看每一段第一句與最後一句，然後看每段中間關鍵字（即考題出現之字）。

A

The kilt is a skirt traditionally worn by Scottish men. It is a tailored garment that is wrapped around the wearer's body at the waist starting from one side, around the front and back and across the front again to the opposite side. The overlapping layers in front are called "aprons." Usually, the kilt covers the body from the waist down to just above the knees. A properly made kilt should not be so loose that the wearer can easily twist the kilt around the body, nor should it be so tight that it causes bulging of the fabric where it is buckled. Underwear may be worn as one prefers.

One of the most distinctive features of the kilt is the pattern of squares, or sett, it exhibits. The association of particular patterns with individual families can be traced back hundreds of years. Then in the Victorian era (19th century), weaving companies began to systematically record and formalize the system of setts for commercial purposes. Today there are also setts for States and Provinces, schools and universities, and general patterns that anybody can wear.

The kilt can be worn with accessories. On the front apron, there is often a kilt pin, topped with a small decorative family symbol. A small knife can be worn with the kilt too. It typically comes in a very wide variety, from fairly plain to quite elaborate silver- and jewel-ornamented designs. The kilt can also be worn with a sporran, which is the Gaelic word for pouch or purse.

1. What's the proper way of wearing the kilt?
   (A) It should be worn with underwear underneath it.
   (B) It should loosely fit on the body to be turned around.
   (C) It should be long enough to cover the wearer's knees.
   (D) It should be wrapped across the front of the body two times.

2. Which of the following is a correct description about setts?
   (A) They were once symbols for different Scottish families.
   (B) They were established by the government for business purposes.
   (C) They represented different States and Provinces in the 19th century.
   (D) They used to come in one general pattern for all individuals and institutions.

3. Which of the following items is **NOT** typically worn with the kilt for decoration?
   (A) A pin.
   (B) A purse.
   (C) A ruby apron.
   (D) A silver knife.

4. What is the purpose of this passage?
   (A) To introduce a Scottish garment.
   (B) To advertise a weaving pattern.
   (C) To persuade men to wear kilts.
   (D) To compare a skirt with a kilt.

Source：101 年大學學測英文閱讀測驗

解答

1. The first paragraph
   Thesis statement (the writer's position / opinion / perspective):
   The kilt is a skirt traditionally worn by Scottish men.

解答

2. The second paragraph
   (1) Topic sentence of 2nd paragraph:
   One of the most distinctive features of the kilt is the pattern of squares, or sett, it exhibits.
   (2) main idea of the 2nd paragraph: the pattern of squares, or sett
   (3) Supporting / development sentences of 2nd paragraph: chronological order
   (4) Concluding sentence: N / A (not applicable)

3. The third paragraph
   (1) Topic sentence of 3rd paragraph:
   The kilt can be worn with accessories.
   (2) main idea of the 3rd paragraph: accessories
   (3) Supporting / development sentences of 3rd paragraph: examples
   (4) Concluding sentence: N / A (not applicable)

本文屬於描述文（description）或說明文（exposition）。

【Answers】

1. (D) (It is a tailored garment that is wrapped around the wearer's body at the waist starting from one side, around the front and back and across the front again to the opposite side.)

2. (A) (The association of particular patterns with individual families can be traced back hundreds of years.)

3. (C) (pin, knife, purse, but not apron)

4. (A) (**The kilt is a skirt traditionally worn by Scottish men.**)

B

Wesla Whitfield, a famous jazz singer, has a unique style and life story, so I decided to see one of her performances and interview her for my column.

I went to a nightclub in New York and watched the stage lights go up. After the band played an introduction, Wesla Whitfield wheeled herself onstage in a wheelchair. As she sang, Whitfield's voice was so powerful and soulful that everyone in the room forgot the wheelchair was even there.

At 57, Whitfield is small and pretty, witty and humble, persistent and philosophical. Raised in California, Whitfield began performing in public at age 18, when she took a job as a singing waitress at a pizza parlor. After studying classical music in college, she moved to San Francisco and went on to sing with the San Francisco Opera Chorus.

Walking home from rehearsal at age 29, she was caught in the midst of a random shooting that left her paralyzed from the waist down. I asked how she dealt with the realization that she'd never walk again, and she confessed that initially she didn't want to face it. After a year of depression she tried to kill herself. She was then admitted to a hospital for treatment, where she was able to recover.

Whitfield said she came to understand that the only thing she had lost in this misfortunate event was the ability to walk. She still possessed her most valuable asset-her mind. Pointing to her head, she said, "Everything important is in here. The only real disability in life is losing your mind." When I asked if she was angry about what she had lost, she admitted to being frustrated occasionally, "especially when everybody's dancing, because I love to dance. But **when that happens** I just remove myself so I can focus instead on what I can do."

1. In which of the following places has Wesla Whitfield worked?
   (A) A college. (B) A hospital.
   (C) A pizza parlor. (D) A news agency.

2. What does "**when that happens**" mean in the last paragraph?
   (A) When Wesla is losing her mind.
   (B) When Wesla is singing on the stage.
   (C) When Wesla is going out in her wheelchair.
   (D) When Wesla is watching other people dancing.

3. Which of the following statements is true about Wesla Whitfield's physical disability?
   (A) It was caused by a traffic accident.
   (B) It made her sad and depressed at first.
   (C) It seriously affected her singing career.
   (D) It happened when she was a college student.

4. What advice would Wesla most likely give other disabled people?
   (A) Ignore what you have lost and make the best use of what you have.
   (B) Be modest and hard-working to earn respect from other people.
   (C) Acquire a skill so that you can still be successful and famous.
   (D) Try to sing whenever you feel upset and depressed.

Source：101 年大學學測英文閱讀測驗

解答

1. The first paragraph

   Thesis statement (the writer's position / opinion / perspective):

   Wesla Whitfield, a famous jazz singer, has a unique style and life story.

2. The second paragraph

   (1) Topic sentence of 2nd paragraph:

   I went to a nightclub in New York and watched the stage lights go up.

   (2) main idea of the 2nd paragraph: a nightclub

   (3) Supporting / development sentences of 2nd paragraph: chronological order

   (4) Concluding sentence: N / A (not applicable)

3. The third paragraph

   (1) Topic sentence of 3rd paragraph:

   At 57, Whitfield is small and pretty, witty and humble, persistent and philosophical.

   (2) main idea of the 3rd paragraph: appearance and characterization

   (3) Supporting / development sentences of 3rd paragraph: chronological order

   (4) Concluding sentence: N / A (not applicable)

4. The fourth paragraph

   (1) Topic sentence of 4th paragraph:

   Walking home from rehearsal at age 29, she was caught in the midst of a random shooting that left her paralyzed from the waist down.

   (2) main idea of the 4th paragraph: caught in the midst of a random shooting

   (3) Supporting / development sentences of 4th paragraph: chronological order

   (4) Concluding sentence: N / A (not applicable)

5. The fifth paragraph

   (1) Topic sentence of 5th paragraph:

   Whitfield said she came to understand that the only thing she had lost in this misfortunate event was the ability to walk.

   (2) main idea of the 5th paragraph: lost the ability to walk

   (3) Supporting / development sentences of 5th paragraph: comparison (walk

解答

and mind)

(4) Concluding sentence: N / A (not applicable)

此篇是典型的時間順序法（chronological order）。

【Answers】

1. (C) (when she took a job as a singing waitress at a pizza parlor.)

2. (D) ("especially when everybody's dancing....)

3. (B) (she confessed that initially she didn't want to face it. After a year of depression she tried to kill herself.)

4. (A) (I just remove myself so I can focus instead on what I can do.")

C

Forks trace their origins back to the ancient Greeks. Forks at that time were fairly large with two tines that aided in the carving of meat in the kitchen. The tines prevented meat from twisting or moving during carving and allowed food to slide off more easily than it would with a knife.

By the 7th century A.D., royal courts of the Middle East began to use forks at the table for dining. From the 10th through the 13th centuries, forks were fairly common among the wealthy in Byzantium. In the 11th century, a Byzantine wife brought forks to Italy; however, they were not widely adopted there until the 16th century. Then in 1533, forks were brought from Italy to France. The French were also slow to accept forks, for using them was thought to be awkward.

In 1608, forks were brought to England by Thomas Coryate, who saw them during his travels in Italy. The English first ridiculed forks as being unnecessary. "Why should a person need a fork when God had given him hands?" they asked. Slowly, however, forks came to be adopted by the wealthy as a symbol of their social status. They were prized possessions made of expensive materials intended to impress guests. By the mid 1600s, eating with forks was considered fashionable among the wealthy British.

Early table forks were modeled after kitchen forks, but small pieces of food often fell through the two tines or slipped off easily. In late 17th century France, larger forks with four curved tines were developed. The additional tines made diners less likely to drop food, and the curved tines served as a scoop so people did not have to constantly switch to a spoon while eating. By the early 19th century, four-tined forks had also been developed in Germany and England and slowly began to spread to America.

1. What is the passage mainly about?
   (A) The different designs of forks.
   (B) The spread of fork-aided cooking.
   (C) The history of using forks for dining.
   (D) The development of fork-related table manners.

2. By which route did the use of forks spread?
   (A) Middle East → Greece → England → Italy → France
   (B) Greece → Middle East → Italy → France → England

(C) Greece → Middle East → France → Italy → Germany

(D) Middle East → France → England → Italy → Germany

3. How did forks become popular in England?

(A) Wealthy British were impressed by the design of forks.

(B) Wealthy British thought it awkward to use their hands to eat.

(C) Wealthy British gave special forks to the nobles as luxurious gifts.

(D) Wealthy British considered dining with forks a sign of social status.

4. Why were forks made into a curved shape?

(A) They could be used to scoop food as well.

(B) They looked more fashionable in this way.

(C) They were designed in this way for export to the US.

(D) They ensured the meat would not twist while being cut.

Source：101 年大學學測英文閱讀測驗

解答

1. The first paragraph

Thesis statement (the writer's position / opinion / perspective):

Forks trace their origins back to the ancient Greeks.

2. The second paragraph

(1) Topic sentence of 2nd paragraph:

By the 7th century A.D., royal courts of the Middle East began to use forks at the table for dining.

(2) main idea of the 2nd paragraph: royal courts began to use forks

(3) Supporting / development sentences of 2nd paragraph: chronological order

解答

(4) Concluding sentence: N / A (not applicable)

3. The third paragraph
   (1) Topic sentence of 3rd paragraph:
   In 1608, forks were brought to England by Thomas Coryate, who saw them during his travels in Italy.
   (2) main idea of the 3rd paragraph: forks were brought to England
   (3) Supporting / development sentences of 3rd paragraph: chronological order
   (4) Concluding sentence: N / A (not applicable)

4. The fourth paragraph
   (1) Topic sentence of 4th paragraph:
   Early table forks were modeled after kitchen forks, but small pieces of food often fell through the two tines or slipped off easily.
   (2) main idea of the 4th paragraph: but small pieces of food often....
   (3) Supporting / development sentences of 4th paragraph: chronological order
   (4) Concluding sentence: N / A (not applicable)

此篇亦是典型的時間順序法（chronological order）。

【Answers】

1. (C) (**Forks trace their origins back to the ancient Greeks.**)

2. (B) (**ancient Greeks, royal courts of the Middle East,** Then in 1533, forks were brought from Italy to France, **In 1608, forks were brought to England by Thomas Coryate.**)

3. (D) (Slowly, however, forks came to be adopted by the wealthy as a symbol of their social status.)

4. (A) (and the curved tines served as a scoop so people did not have to constantly switch to a spoon while eating.)

D

Animals are a favorite subject of many photographers. Cats, dogs, and other pets top the list, followed by zoo animals. However, because it's hard to get them to sit still and "perform on command," some professional photographers refuse to photograph pets.

One way to get an appealing portrait of a cat or dog is to hold a biscuit or treat above the camera. The animal's longing look toward the food will be captured by the camera, but the treat won't appear in the picture because it's out of the camera's range. When you show the picture to your friends afterwards, they'll be impressed by your pet's loving expression.

If you are using fast film, you can take some good, quick shots of a pet by simply snapping a picture right after calling its name. You'll get a different expression from your pet using this technique. Depending on your pet's mood, the picture will capture an interested, curious expression or possibly a look of annoyance, especially if you've awakened it from a nap.

Taking pictures of zoo animals requires a little more patience. After all, you can't wake up a lion! You may have to wait for a while until the animal does something interesting or moves into a position for you to get a good shot. When photographing zoo animals, don't get too close to the cages, and never tap on the glass or throw things between the bars of a cage. Concentrate on shooting some good pictures, and always respect the animals you are photographing.

1. Why do some professional photographers **NOT** like to take pictures of pets?
   (A) Pets may not follow orders.
   (B) Pets don't want to be bothered.
   (C) Pets may not like photographers.
   (D) Pets seldom change their expressions.

2. What is the use of a biscuit in taking pictures of a pet?
   (A) To capture a cute look.
   (B) To create a special atmosphere.
   (C) To arouse the appetite of the pet.
   (D) To keep the pet from looking at the camera.

3. What is the advantage of calling your pet's name when taking a shot of it?
   (A) To help your pet look its best.
   (B) To make sure that your pet sits still.
   (C) To keep your pet awake for a while.
   (D) To catch a different expression of your pet.

4. In what way is photographing zoo animals different from photographing pets?
   (A) You need to have fast film.
   (B) You need special equipment.
   (C) You need to stay close to the animals.
   (D) You need more time to watch and wait.

Source：101 年大學學測英文閱讀測驗

解答

1. The first paragraph
   Thesis statement (the writer's position / opinion / perspective):
   Animals are a favorite subject of many photographers.

2. The second paragraph
   (1) Topic sentence of 2nd paragraph:
   One way to get an appealing portrait of a cat or dog is to hold a biscuit or treat above the camera.
   (2) main idea of the 2nd paragraph: hold a biscuit or treat
   (3) Supporting / development sentences of 2nd paragraph: technique
   (4) Concluding sentence: N / A (not applicable)

3. The third paragraph
   (1) Topic sentence of 3rd paragraph:
   If you are using fast film, you can take some good, quick shots of a pet by simply snapping a picture right after calling its name.
   (2) main idea of the 3rd paragraph: calling its name
   (3) Supporting / development sentences of 3rd paragraph: another technique (calling its name)
   (4) Concluding sentence: N / A (not applicable)

4. The fourth paragraph
   (1) Topic sentence of 4th paragraph:
   Taking pictures of zoo animals requires a little more patience.
   (2) main idea of the 4th paragraph: patience
   (3) Supporting / development sentences of 4th paragraph: example
   (4) Concluding sentence: N / A (not applicable)

本文屬於描述（description）或說明文（exposition），說明寵物照相的方法。

【Answers】

1. (A) (because it's hard to get them to sit still and "perform on command,")

解答

2. (A) (**One way to get an appealing portrait of a cat or dog....**)

3. (D) (You'll get a different expression from your pet using this technique.)

4. (D) (**Taking pictures of zoo animals requires a little more patience.**)

E

There is a long-held belief that when meeting someone, the more eye contact we have with the person, the better. The result is an unfortunate tendency for people making initial contact-in a job interview, for example-to stare fixedly at the other individual. However, this behavior is likely to make the interviewer feel very uncomfortable. Most of us are comfortable with eye contact lasting a few seconds. But eye contact which persists longer than that can make us nervous.

Another widely accepted belief is that powerful people in a society-often men-show their dominance over others by touching them in a variety of ways. In fact, research shows that in almost all cases, lower-status people initiate touch. Women also initiate touch more often than men do.

The belief that rapid speech and lying go together is also widespread and enduring. We react strongly-and suspiciously-to fast talk. However, the opposite is a greater cause for suspicion. Speech that is slow, because it is laced with pauses or errors, is a more reliable indicator of lying than the opposite.

1. Which of the following statements is true according to the passage?
   (A) Rapid speech without mistakes is a reliable sign of intelligence.
   (B) Women often play a more dominant role than men in a community.
   (C) Speaking slowly is more often a sign of lying than speaking quickly.
   (D) Touching tends to be initiated first by people of higher social positions.

2. What is true about fixing your eyes on a person when you first meet him / her?
   (A) Fixing your eyes on the person will make him / her feel at ease.
   (B) It is more polite to fix your eyes on him / her as long as you can.
   (C) Most people feel uneasy to have eye contact for over a few seconds.
   (D) It doesn't make a difference whether you fix your eyes on him / her or not.

3. Which of the following is **NOT** discussed in the passage?
   (A) Facial expressions.
   (B) Physical contact.
   (C) Rate of speech.
   (D) Eye contact.

4. What is the main idea of the passage?
   (A) People have an instinct for interpreting non-verbal communication.
   (B) We should not judge the intention of a person by his body

language.

(C) A good knowledge of body language is essential for successful communication.

(D) Common beliefs about verbal and non-verbal communication are not always correct.

Source：100年大學學測英文閱讀測驗

解答

1. The first paragraph

   Thesis statement (the writer's position / opinion / perspective):

   There is a long-held belief that when meeting someone, the more eye contact we have with the person, the better.

2. The second paragraph

   (1) Topic sentence of 2nd paragraph:

   Another widely accepted belief is that powerful people in a society-often men-show their dominance over others by touching them in a variety of ways.

   (2) main idea of the 2nd paragraph: another accepted belief

   (3) Supporting / development sentences of 2nd paragraph: research evidence

   (4) Concluding sentence: N / A (not applicable)

3. The third paragraph

   (1) Topic sentence of 3rd paragraph:

   The belief that rapid speech and lying go together is also widespread and enduring.

   (2) main idea of the 3rd paragraph: rapid speech and lying

   (3) Supporting / development sentences of 3rd paragraph: comparison

   (4) Concluding sentence: N / A (not applicable)

本文屬於描述（description）或說明文（exposition）。

解答

【Answers】

1. (C) (Speech that is slow, because it is laced with pauses or errors, is a more reliable indicator of lying than the opposite.)

2. (C) (But eye contact which persists longer than that can make us nervous.)

3. (A) (It is not discussed.)

4. (D) (However, In fact, However)

F

It is easy for us to tell our friends from our enemies. But can other animals do the same? **Elephants can!** They can use their sense of vision and smell to tell the difference between people who pose a threat and those who do not.

In Kenya, researchers found that elephants react differently to clothing worn by men of the Maasai and Kamba ethnic groups. Young Maasai men spear animals and thus pose a threat to elephants; Kamba men are mainly farmers and are not a danger to elephants.

In an experiment conducted by animal scientists, elephants were first presented with clean clothing or clothing that had been worn for five days by either a Maasai or a Kamba man. When the elephants detected the smell of clothing worn by a Maasai man, they moved away from the smell faster and took longer to relax than when they detected the smells of either clothing worn by Kamba men or clothing that had not been worn at all.

Garment color also plays a role, though in a different way. In the same study, when the elephants saw red clothing not worn before, they reacted angrily, as red is typically worn by Maasai men. Rather than running away as they did with the smell, the elephants acted aggressively toward the red clothing.

The researchers believe that the elephants' emotional reactions are due to their different interpretations of the smells and the sights. Smelling a potential danger means that a threat is nearby and the best thing to do is run away and hide. Seeing a potential threat without its smell means that risk is low. Therefore, instead of showing fear and running away, the elephants express their anger and become aggressive.

1. According to the passage, which of the following statements is true about Kamba and Maasai people?
   (A) Maasai people are a threat to elephants.
   (B) Kamba people raise elephants for farming.
   (C) Both Kamba and Maasai people are elephant hunters.
   (D) Both Kamba and Maasai people traditionally wear red clothing.

2. How did the elephants react to smell in the study?
   (A) They attacked a man with the smell of new clothing.
   (B) They needed time to relax when smelling something unfamiliar.
   (C) They became anxious when they smelled Kamba-scented clothing.
   (D) They were frightened and ran away when they smelled their enemies.

3. What is the main idea of this passage?
   (A) Elephants use sight and smell to detect danger.
   (B) Elephants attack people who wear red clothing.
   (C) Scientists are now able to control elephants' emotions.
   (D) Some Kenyan tribes understand elephants' emotions very well.

4. What can be inferred about the elephant's behavior from this passage?
   (A) Elephants learn from their experiences.
   (B) Elephants have sharper sense of smell than sight.
   (C) Elephants are more intelligent than other animals.
   (D) Elephants tend to attack rather than escape when in danger.

Source：100 年大學學測英文閱讀測驗

解答

1. The first paragraph
   Thesis statement (the writer's position / opinion / perspective):
   Elephants can tell the difference between people who pose a threat and those who do not.

2. The second paragraph
   (1) Topic sentence of 2nd paragraph:
   In Kenya, researchers found that elephants react differently to clothing worn by men of the Maasai and Kamba ethnic groups.
   (2) main idea of the 2nd paragraph: elephants react differently
   (3) Supporting / development sentences of 2nd paragraph: comparison
   (4) Concluding sentence: N / A (not applicable)

3. The third paragraph

解答

(1) Topic sentence of 3rd paragraph:

In an experiment conducted by animal scientists, elephants were first presented with clean clothing or clothing that had been worn for five days by either a Maasai or a Kamba man.

(2) main idea of the 3rd paragraph: an experiment

(3) Supporting / development sentences of 3rd paragraph: comparison

(4) Concluding sentence: N / A (not applicable)

4. The fourth paragraph

(1) Topic sentence of 4th paragraph:

Garment color also plays a role, though in a different way.

(2) main idea of the 4th paragraph: garment color

(3) Supporting / development sentences of 4th paragraph: comparison

(4) Concluding sentence: N / A (not applicable)

5. The fifth paragraph

(1) Topic sentence of 5th paragraph:

The researchers believe that the elephants' emotional reactions are due to their different interpretations of the smells and the sights.

(2) main idea of the 5th paragraph: different interpretations of the smells and the sights

(3) Supporting / development sentences of 5th paragraph: smelling, seeing

(4) Concluding sentence: N / A (not applicable)

本文屬於描述（description）或說明文（exposition）。

【Answers】

1. (A) (Young Maasai men spear animals and thus pose a threat to elephants;)

2. (D) (When the elephants detected the smell of clothing worn by a Maasai man, they moved away from the smell faster and took longer to relax....)

3. (A) (They can use their sense of vision and smell to tell the difference between people who pose a threat and those who do not.)

解答

4. (A) (**The researchers believe that the elephants' emotional reactions are due to their different interpretations of the smells and the sights.**)

G

It was something she had dreamed of since she was five. Finally, after years of training and intensive workouts, Deborah Duffey was going to compete in her first high school basketball game. The goals of becoming an outstanding player and playing college ball were never far from Deborah's mind.

The game was against Mills High School. With 1:42 minutes left in the game, Deborah's team led by one point. A player of Mills had possession of the ball, and Deborah ran to guard against her. As Deborah shuffled sideways to block the player, her knee went out and she collapsed on the court in burning pain. Just like that, Deborah's season was over.

After suffering the bad injury, Deborah found that, for the first time in her life, she was in a situation beyond her control. Game after game, she could do nothing but sit on the sidelines watching others play the game that she loved so much.

Injuries limited Deborah's time on the court as she hurt her knees three more times in the next five years. She had to spend countless hours in a physical therapy clinic to receive treatment. Her frequent visits there gave her a passion and respect for the profession. And Deborah began to see a new light in her life.

Currently a senior in college, Deborah focuses on pursuing a degree in physical therapy. After she graduates, Deborah plans to use her knowledge to educate people how to best take care of their bodies and cope with the feelings of hopelessness that she remembers so well.

1. What is the best title for this passage?
   (A) A Painful Mistake (B) A Great Adventure
   (C) A Lifelong Punishment (D) A New Direction in Life

2. How did Deborah feel when she first hurt her knee?
   (A) Excited. (B) Confused.
   (C) Ashamed. (D) Disappointed.

3. What is true about Deborah Duffey?
   (A) She didn't play on the court after the initial injury.
   (B) She injured her knee when she was trying to block her opponent.
   (C) She knew that she couldn't be a basketball player when she was a child.
   (D) She refused to seek professional assistance to help her recover from her injuries.

4. What was the new light that Deborah saw in her life?
   (A) To help people take care of their bodies.
   (B) To become a teacher of Physical Education.
   (C) To become an outstanding basketball player.
   (D) To receive treatment in a physical therapy office.

Source：100 年大學學測英文閱讀測驗

解答

1. The first paragraph
   Thesis statement (the writer's position / opinion / perspective):
   It was something she had dreamed of since she was five.

2. The second paragraph
   (1) Topic sentence of 2nd paragraph:
   The game was against Mills High School.
   (2) main idea of the 2nd paragraph: the game was against Mills High School
   (3) Supporting / development sentences of 2nd paragraph: description
   (4) Concluding sentence: N / A (not applicable)

3. The third paragraph
   (1) Topic sentence of 3rd paragraph:
   After suffering the bad injury, Deborah found that, for the first time in her life, she was in a situation beyond her control.
   (2) main idea of the 3rd paragraph: she was in a situation beyond her control
   (3) Supporting / development sentences of 3rd paragraph: description
   (4) Concluding sentence: N / A (not applicable)

4. The fourth paragraph
   (1) Topic sentence of 4th paragraph:
   Injuries limited Deborah's time on the court as she hurt her knees three more times in the next five years.
   (2) main idea of the 4th paragraph: injuries
   (3) Supporting / development sentences of 4th paragraph: turning point
   (4) Concluding sentence: N / A (not applicable)

5. The fifth paragraph
   (1) Topic sentence of 5th paragraph:
   Currently a senior in college, Deborah focuses on pursuing a degree in physical therapy.
   (2) main idea of the 5th paragraph: focusing on a degree in physical therapy
   (3) Supporting / development sentences of 5th paragraph: turning point

解答

(4) Concluding sentence: N / A (not applicable)

本文屬於描述（description）或說明文（exposition）。

【Answers】

1. (D) (And Deborah began to see a new light in her life.)

2. (D) (**After suffering the bad injury, Deborah found that, for the first time in her life, she was in a situation beyond her control.**)

3. (B) (As Deborah shuffled sideways to block the player, her knee went out and she collapsed on the court in burning pain.)

4. (A) (After she graduates, Deborah plans to use her knowledge to educate people how to best take care of their bodies....)

H

Redwood trees are the tallest plants on the earth, reaching heights of up to 100 meters. They are also known for their longevity, typically 500 to 1000 years, but sometimes more than 2000 years. A hundred million years ago, in the age of dinosaurs, redwoods were common in the forests of a much more moist and tropical North America. As the climate became drier and colder, they retreated to a narrow strip along the Pacific coast of Northern California.

The trunk of redwood trees is very stout and usually forms a single straight column. It is covered with a beautiful soft, spongy bark. This bark can be pretty thick, well over two feet in the more mature trees. It gives the older trees a certain kind of protection from insects, but the main benefit is that it keeps the center of the tree intact from moderate forest fires because of its thickness. This fire resistant quality explains why the giant redwood grows to live that long. While most other types of trees are destroyed by forest fires, the giant redwood actually prospers because of them. Moderate fires will clear the ground of competing plant life, and the rising heat dries and opens the ripe cones of the redwood, releasing many thousands of seeds onto the ground below.

New trees are often produced from sprouts, little baby trees, which form at the base of the trunk. These sprouts grow slowly, nourished by the root system of the "mother" tree. When the main tree dies, the sprouts are then free to grow as full trees, forming a "**fairy ring**" of trees around the initial tree. These trees, in turn, may give rise to more sprouts, and the cycle continues.

1. Why were redwood trees more prominent in the forests of North America millions of years ago?
   (A) The trees were taller and stronger.
   (B) The soil was softer for seeds to sprout.
   (C) The climate was warmer and more humid.
   (D) The temperature was lower along the Pacific coast.

2. What does a "**fairy ring**" in the last paragraph refer to?
   (A) Circled tree trunks.
   (B) Connected root systems.
   (C) Insect holes around an old tree.
   (D) Young trees surrounding a mature tree.

3. Which of the following is a function of the tree bark as mentioned in the passage?
   (A) It allows redwood trees to bear seeds.
   (B) It prevents redwood trees from attack by insects.
   (C) It helps redwood trees absorb moisture in the air.
   (D) It makes redwood trees more beautiful and appealing.

4. Why do redwood trees grow to live that long according to the passage?
   (A) They have heavy and straight tree trunks.
   (B) They are properly watered and nourished.
   (C) They are more resistant to fire damage than other trees.
   (D) They produce many young trees to sustain their life cycle.

Source：100 年大學學測英文閱讀測驗

解答

1. The first paragraph
   Thesis statement (the writer's position / opinion / perspective):
   Redwood trees are the tallest plants on the earth, reaching heights of up to 100 meters.

2. The second paragraph
   (1) Topic sentence of 2nd paragraph:
   The trunk of redwood trees is very stout and usually forms a single straight column.
   (2) main idea of the 2nd paragraph: trunk is stout and forms a single straight column
   (3) Supporting / development sentences of 2nd paragraph: description, comparison
   (4) Concluding sentence: N / A (not applicable)

解答

3. The third paragraph
   (1) Topic sentence of 3rd paragraph:
   New trees are often produced from sprouts, little baby trees, which form at the base of the trunk.
   (2) main idea of the 3rd paragraph: new trees
   (3) Supporting / development sentences of 3rd paragraph: cycle
   (4) Concluding sentence: N / A (not applicable)

本文屬於描述（description）或說明文（exposition）。

【Answers】

1. (C) (redwoods were common in the forests of a much more moist and tropical North America.)

2. (D) (When the main tree dies, the sprouts are then free to grow as full trees, forming a "**fairy ring**" of trees around the initial tree.)

3. (B) (It gives the older trees a certain kind of protection from insects,)

4. (C) (This fire resistant quality explains why the giant redwood grows to live that long.)

I

Falling in love is always magical. It feels eternal as if love will last ___31___. We naively believe that somehow we are ___32___ from the problems our parents had. We are assured that we are destined to live happily ever after.

But as the magic fades and daily life ___33___, it happens that men, forgetting that men and women are supposed to be different, continue to expect women to think and react the way men do; women, ___34___, expect men to feel and behave the way women do. ___35___ taking time to understand and respect each other, we become demanding, resentful, judgmental, and intolerant.

___36___, our relationships are filled with unnecessary disagreements and conflicts. Somehow, problems creep in, resentments build, and communication ___37___. Mistrust increases and rejection and repression surface. The magic of love is then lost.

Very ___38___ people are able to grow in love. Yet, it does happen. ___39___ men and women are able to respect and accept their differences, love has a chance to blossom. Love is, ___40___, magical, and it certainly can last if we remember our differences and respect each other.

(A) breaks down (B) Consequently (C) similarly (D) indeed
(E) few (F) forever (G) Instead of (H) takes over (I) free
(J) As long as

Source：94 年大學學測

解答

31. (F) forever

32. (I) free

33. (H) takes over

34. (C) similary

35. (G) Instead of

解答

36. (B) Consequently

37. (A) breaks down

38. (E) few

39. (J) As long as

40. (D) indeed

- **Introduction（引言段）：**

  Thesis Statement：Falling in love is always magical.（戀愛總是具有魔力；戀愛總是迷人的）。

- **第二段：**

  主題句：But as the magic fades and daily life takes over....。

  中心思想（關鍵字）：magic fades。

  闡述句策略：中間掃描比較法（similarly, men and women）。

  結論句：Instead of taking time to understand and respect each other, we become demanding, resentful, judgmental, and intolerant.

- **第三段：**

  主題句：Consequently, our relationships are filled with unnecessary disagreements and conflicts.

  中心思想（關鍵字）：disagreements and conflicts。

  闡述句策略：中間掃描描述法（Somehow, problems creep in....）。

  結論句：The magic of love is then lost.

- **Conclusion（結論段）：**

  Thesis statement：Love is, indeed, magical, and it certainly can last if we remember our differences and respect each other.（愛

情真的是有魔力的；如果我們記得我們的差異並尊重彼此，如此愛情一定能夠持續）。

大學指考閱讀測驗

A

Jean Piaget, a psychologist and pioneer in the study of child intelligence, was born in Switzerland in 1896. At **age 10**, he managed his first __26__, a description of a partly albino sparrow he observed in a public park. At **age 15**, he __27__ to devote his life to developing a biological explanation of knowledge.

He began his career as a zoologist, __28__ mollusks and their adaptations to their environment. __29__ **age 21**, he had already published 25 professional papers on that topic. Later, after working with Alfred Binet in Paris, he became interested in levels of logic used by children taking standardized tests on intelligence. Piaget __30__ to establish a body of psychology all his life and became a very influential figure in educational psychology. His works were all written originally in French and were later translated into English.

26. (A) subscription (B) publication
    (C) obligation (D) transaction
27. (A) put down (B) passed on
    (C) ended up (D) set out
28. (A) study (B) studied
    (C) studying (D) being studied

29. (A) By　　(B) In
(C) With　　(D) On
30. (A) forgot　　(B) afforded
(C) sought　　(D) tended

Source：94 年大學指考

解答

26. (B), 27. (D), 28. (C), 29. (A), 30. (C)

- **主題句：**Jean Piaget, a psychologist and pioneer in the study of child intelligence, was born in Switzerland in 1896.
- **中心思想（關鍵字）：**Jean Piaget。
- **發展句策略：**時間順序法（age 10, age 15, age 21）。
- **結論句：**His works were all written originally in French and were later translated into English.
- **大意：**皮亞傑於 1896 年在瑞士誕生，在兒童智商領域方面是個心理學家與先驅。接著作者以時間順序法說明皮亞傑的學術發展經過。

B

Average global temperature has increased by almost 1° F over the past century. Scientists expect it to increase an additional 2° to 6° F over the next one hundred years. This may not sound like much, but it could change the Earth's climate as never before.

Climate change may **affect** people's health both directly and indirectly. For instance, heat stress and other heat-related health problems

are caused directly by very warm temperatures. Indirectly, human health **can also be affected** by ecological disturbances, changes in food and water supplies, as well as coastal flooding. How people and nature adapt to climate change will determine how seriously it **affects** human health. Generally, poor people and poor countries are less probable to have the money and resources they need to cope with health problems due to climate change.

Source：96 / 92 年大學指考

- **主題句：**Climate change may affect people's health both directly and indirectly。
- **中心思想（關鍵字）：**affect。
- **闡述句策略：**因果法（are caused by, can also be affected by, due to）。
- **結論句：**Generally, poor people and poor countries are less probable to have the money and resources they need to cope with health problems due to climate change.
- **大意：**氣候改變可能直接與間接影響人們的健康。接著作者以因果法說明直接與間接的影響。

C

Europe, on the whole, has the **world's most restrictive laws** on animal experiments. Even so, its scientists use some 12 million animals a year, most of them mice and rats, for medical research. Official statistics show that just 1.1 million animals are used in research in **America** each year. But that is misleading. The American authorities do not think mice and rats are worth counting and, as these are the most common laboratory animals, the true figure is much **higher**. **Japan** and **China** have even **less comprehensive data** than America.

Source：100 年大學指考

- **主題句：**Europe, on the whole, has the world's most restrictive laws on animal experiments.
- **中心思想（關鍵字）：**most restrictive laws。
- **發展句策略：**比較法（America, higher, Japan and China have less comprehensive data than America）。
- **結論句：**N / A。
- **大意：**整體而言，在動物實驗的法律方面，歐洲是世界上限制最嚴格的地區。接著作者以比較法比較美國、日本與中國的資料。

D

Children's encounters with poetry should include **three types of response-enjoyment, exploration, and deepening understanding**. These do not occur always as ___21___ steps but may happen simultaneously. Certainly, children must start with **enjoyment** ___22___ their interest in poetry dies. But if from the beginning they find delight in the poems they hear or read, they are ready and eager to ___23___ further-more books and more poems of different sorts. Even the youngest children can learn to see implications ___24___ the obvious. To read for hidden meanings is to identify with the poet, to ask the poet's questions. This is reading for **deeper understanding**,

___25___ a thoughtful look at what lies beneath the surface. **Enjoyment, exploration, and deeper understanding** must all be part of children's experience with poetry if we are to help them to love it.

21. (A) childish (B) artistic (C) separate (D) innocent
22. (A) or (B) and (C) so (D) then
23. (A) escape (B) explore (C) accustom (D) appear
24. (A) near (B) among (C) beyond (D) without
25. (A) take (B) takes (C) to take (D) taking

Source：93 年大學指考

解答

21. (C), 22. (A), 23. (B), 24. (C), 25. (D)

- **主題句：**Children's encounters with poetry should include three types of response-enjoyment, exploration, and deepening understanding.
- **中心思想（關鍵字）：**three types of response。
- **發展句策略：**分類法（enjoyment, exploration, deepening understanding）。
- **結論句：**Enjoyment, exploration, and deeper understanding must all be part of children's experience with poetry if we are to help them to love it.

• **大意：**孩子們與詩接觸時，應該包含三種反應——樂趣、探索與加深的領會。接著作者以分類法依序說明此三種反應。

E

If old newspapers are stacking up in your house, there are **options** other than tossing them out or selling them to a recycler. Some environmental scientists **suggest** turning newspapers __16__ charcoal. This can be done by soaking sheets of newspaper in water for two hours and then __17__ them into small pieces. These pieces are then compressed into balls. After the water is __18__, the ball-shaped pieces are put under the sun to dry before they can be used as a firewood or charcoal substitute. __19__ **suggestion** made by the experts is to dip newspaper sheets in vinegar and water, and use them to clean windows, mirrors, and tiles. Old papers can __20__ be used to line rubbish bins and as packing material when mailing breakable goods.

16. (A) into　(B) for
    (C) off　(D) upon
17. (A) tear　(B) tore
    (C) tearing　(D) torn
18. (A) boiled down　(B) fired up
    (C) kicked off　(D) squeezed out
19. (A) This　(B) Another
    (C) That　(D) Other
20. (A) soon　(B) also
    (C) thus　(D) rather

Source：93 年大學指考

解答

16. (A), 17. (C), 18. (D), 19. (B), 20. (B)

- **主題句：**If old newspapers are stacking up in your house, there are options other than tossing them out or selling them to a recycler.
- **中心思想（關鍵字）：**options。
- **闡述句策略：**問題解決法（suggest, suggestion）。
- **結論句：**N / A。
- **大意：**如果舊報紙正在你屋中成堆的堆起來，除了將它們扔掉與賣給回收者以外，還有一些選擇。接著作者提供二個建議。

F

Textese (also known as chatspeak, texting language, or txt talk) is a term for the abbreviations and slang most commonly used among young people today. The ___21___ of textese is largely due to the necessary brevity of mobile phone text messaging, though its use is also very common on the Internet, including e-mail and instant messaging.

There are no ___22___ rules for writing textese. However, the common practice is to use single letters, pictures, or numbers to represent whole words. For example, "i < 3 u" uses the picture ___23___ of a heart "< 3" for "love," and the letter "u" to ___24___ "you." For words which have no common abbreviation, textese users often ___25___ the vowels from a word, and the reader is forced to interpret a string of consonants by re-adding the vowels. Thus, "dictionary" becomes "dctnry," and "keyboard" becomes “kybrd.” The reader must interpret the __26__ words depending on the context in which it is used, as there are many examples of words or phrases which use the same abbreviations. So if someone says “ttyl, lol” they probably mean “talk to you later, lots of love” not “talk to you later, laugh out loud,” and if someone says “omg, lol” they most __27__ mean “oh my god, laugh out loud” not “oh my god, lots of love."

The emergence of textese is clearly due to a desire to type less and to communicate more __28__ than one can manage without such shortcuts. Yet it has been severely __29__ as “wrecking our language.” Some scholars even consider the use of textese as “irritating” and essentially lazy behavior. They’re worried that “sloppy” habits gained while using textese will result in students’ growing __30__ of proper spelling, grammar and punctuation.

(A) quickly
(B) criticized
(C) likely
(D) abbreviated
(E) replace
(F) remove
(G) standard
(H) ignorance
(I) popularity
(J) symbol

Source：99 年大學指考

解答

21. (I) popularity

22. (G) standard

23. (J) symbol

解答

24. (E) replace

25. (F) remove

26. (D) abbreviated

27. (C) likely

28. (A) quickly

29. (B) criticized

30. (H) ignorance

- **Introduction（引言段）：**

Thesis Statement：The popularity of textese is largely due to the necessary brevity of mobile phone text messaging, though its use is also very common on the Internet, including e-mail and instant messaging.（簡訊語的普及主要是因為手機簡訊需要簡短，而它的使用在網際網路上也非常普遍，包括電子郵件與即時傳訊）。

- **第二段：**

主題句：There are no standard rules for writing textese. However, the common practice is to use single letters, pictures, or numbers to represent whole words.

中心思想（關鍵字）：no standard rules。

闡述句策略：中間掃描例證法（For example）。

結論句：N / A。

- **Conclusion（結論段）：**

Thesis statement：The emergence of textese is clearly due to a desire to type less and to communicate more quickly than one can manage without such shortcuts.（簡訊語的出現很清楚地是因為需要少打一些字與更快溝通）。

研究所考試閱讀測驗

A

Fossils are the remains and **traces** (such as footprints or other marks) of ancient plant and animal life that are more than 10,000 years old. They range in size from microscopic structures to dinosaur skeletons and complete bodies of enormous animals. Skeletons of extinct species of humans are also considered fossils.

An environment favorable to the growth and later preservation of organisms is required for the occurrence of fossils. Two conditions are almost present: (1) The possession of hard parts, either internal or external, such as bones, teeth, scales, shells, and wood. These parts remain after the rest of the organism has decayed. Organisms that lack hard parts, such as worms and jellyfish, have left a **meager** geologic record. (2) Quick burial of the dead organism, so that protection is afforded against weathering, bacterial action, and scavengers.

Nature provides many situations in which the remains of animals and plants are protected against destruction. **Of these, marine sediment**

is by far the most important environment for the preservations of fossils, owing to the incredible richness of marine life. The beds of former lakes are also prolific sources of fossils. The rapidly accumulating sediments in the channels, floodplains, and deltas of streams bury fresh-water organisms, along with land plants and animals that fall into the water. The beautifully preserved fossil fish from the Green River oil shale of Wyoming in the western United States lived in a vast shallow lake.

The frigid ground in the far north acts as a remarkable preservative for animal fossils. **The woolly mammoth**, a long-haired rhinoceros, and other mammals have been periodically **exposed** in the tundra of Siberia, the hair and red flesh still frozen in cold storage.

Volcanoes often provide environments favorable to fossils preservation. Extensive falls of volcanic ash and coarser particles overwhelm and bury all forms of life, from flying insects to great trees.

Caves have preserved the bones of many animals that died in them and were subsequently buried under a blanket of clay or a cover of dripstone. Predatory animals and early humans alike sought shelter in caves and brought food to **them** to be eaten, leaving bones that paleontologists have discovered.

1. All of the following facts about fossils are referred to by the author in paragraph 1 EXCEPT the fact that they can be ________.
   (A) microscopically small
   (B) skeletons of human ancestors

(C) fragile

(D) complete animal bodies

2. The word "traces" in the passage (in line 1, paragraph 1) is closet in meaning to __________.

(A) structures (B) imprints (C) importance (D) skeletons

3. Which of the following is LEAST likely to be found as a fossil, assuming that all are buried rapidly?

(A) a worm (B) a dinosaur

(C) a woolly mammoth (D) a human ancestor

4. The word "meager" in the passage (in line 5, paragraph 2) is closest in meaning to __________.

(A) great (B) little (C) different (D) vital

5. The fossil fish from the Green River were probably preserved because they were __________.

(A) in a deep lake (B) covered by sediment

(C) buried slowly (D) protected by oil

6. Which of the following best expresses the essential information in the highlighted sentence (in paragraph 3)? *Incorrect* answer choices change the meaning in important ways or leave out essential information.

(A) As plants and animals in marine sediment are incredible, it is easy to preserve fossils in this most important environment.

(B) Sea sediment is far from the most important environment for the preservation of fossils because of the incredible marine plants and animals.

(C) As there are a great number of plants and animals in the sea, marine sediments become the most important environment for preserving fossils.

(D) Sea sediment is surely the most important environment for the preservation of fossils because plants and animals grow in the incredibly rich sea.

7. The author mentions "the woolly mammoth" in the passage (in line 2, paragraph 4) in order to __________.
   (A) illustrate that frigid ground preserves animal fossils
   (B) explain why animals survived in frigid environments
   (C) show how the animals acted as a remarkable preservative
   (D) demonstrate that large animals lived in the far north of the Earth

8. The word "exposed" in the passage (in line 3, paragraph 4) is closest in meaning to __________.
   (A) uncovered (B) photographed
   (C) located (D) preserved

9. It can be inferred from the passage that a condition that favors fossilization when volcanic ash falls to Earth is __________.
   (A) cold storage (B) high temperature
   (C) lack of water (D) quick burial

10. The word "them" in the passage (in line 3, paragraph 6) refers to __________.

(A) predatory animals　　(B) caves
(C) early humans　　(D) bones

Source：雲科大 99 學年度碩士班招生考試試題

解答

1. (C) fragile 易碎的；脆的；易損壞的
2. (B) imprints 痕跡（traces 痕跡）
3. (A) a worm 蟲
4. (B) little（meager 不足的；貧乏的）
5. (D) protected by oil
6. (C) As there are a great number of plants and animals in the sea, marine sediments become the most important environment for preserving fossils.
7. (A) illustrate that frigid ground preserves animal fossils
8. (A) uncovered 未遮蓋的（exposed 暴露的；無遮蔽的）
9. (D) quick burial 快速埋葬
10. (B) caves 洞穴（them）

- **Introduction（引言段）：**

Thesis Statement：Fossils are the remains and **traces** (such as footprints or other marks) of ancient plant and animal life that are more than 10,000 years old.（化石是古代超過一萬年以上植物與動物生命的遺跡與痕跡（譬如腳印或其他的印記）。

- **第二段：**

主題句：An environment favorable to the growth and later preservation of organisms is required for the occurrence of fossils.

中心思想（關鍵字）：environment, the occurrence of fossils。

闡述句策略：中間掃描描述法（two conditions）。

結論句：N / A。

- **第三段：**

主題句：Nature provides many situations in which the remains of animals and plants are protected against destruction.

中心思想（關鍵字）：nature, situations。

闡述句策略：中間掃描例證法（marine sediment, beds of former lakes, Green River oil shale）。

結論句：N / A。

- **第四段：**

主題句：The frigid ground in the far north acts as a remarkable preservative for animal fossils.

中心思想（關鍵字）：frigid ground （嚴寒的地面），preservative。

闡述句策略：中間掃描例證法（the wooly mammoth，長毛象）。

結論句：N / A。

- **第五段：**

主題句：Volcanoes often provide environments favorable to fossils preservation.

中心思想（關鍵字）：volcanoes, environment。

闡述句策略：中間掃描描述法（Extensive falls of volcanic ash and

coarser particles....）。

結論句： N / A。

- **第六段：**

主題句： Caves have preserved the bones of many animals that died in them and were subsequently buried under a blanket of clay or a cover of dripstone.

中心思想（關鍵字）： caves, the bones of many animals。

闡述句策略： 中間掃描描述法（predatory animals and early humans alike）。

結論句： N / A。

- **Conclusion（結論段）：** N / A。

B

Each advance in microscopic technique has provided scientists with new perspectives on the function of living organisms and the nature of matter itself. The invention of the visible-light microscope late in the sixteenth century introduced a previously unknown realm of single-celled plants and animals. In the twentieth century, electron microscopes have provided direct views of viruses and **minuscule** surface structures. Now another type of microscope, one that utilized X-ray microscope rather than light or electrons, offers a different way of examining tiny details; **it** should extend human perception still farther into the natural world.

The dream of building an X-ray microscope dates to 1895. **Its development, however, was virtually halted in the 1940's because the development of the electron microscope was progressing rapidly**.

During the 1940's electron microscopes routinely achieved resolution better than that possible with a visible-light microscope, while the performance of X-ray microscope resisted improvement. In recent years, however, interest in X-ray microscopes has revived, largely because of advances such as the development of new sources of X-ray illumination. As a result, the brightness available today is millions of times that of X-ray tubes, which, for most of the century, were the only available sources of soft X-ray.

The new X-ray microscopes **considerably** improve on the resolution provided by optical microscopes. They can also be used to map the distribution of certain chemical elements. Some can form pictures in extremely short times; others hold the promise of special capabilities such as three-dimensional imaging. Unlike conventional electron microscopy, X-ray microscopy enables specimens to be kept in air and in water. The illumination used, so-called soft X-rays in the wavelength range of twenty to forty angstroms (an angstrom is one ten-billionth of a meter), is also sufficiently penetrating to image intact biological cells in many cases. Because of the wavelength of the X-rays used, soft X-ray microscopes will never match the highest resolution possible with electron microscopes. **Rather**, their special properties will make possible investigations that will complement **those** performed with light - and electron - based instruments.

1. According to the passage (paragraph 1), the invention of the visible-light microscope allowed scientists to ________.
   (A) develop the electron microscope later on

(B) discover single-celled plants and animals they had never seen before

(C) see viruses directly

(D) understand more about the distribution of the chemical elements

2. The word “minuscule” in the passage (in line 5, paragraph 1) is closest in meaning to ________.

(A) circular (B) dangerous (C) tiny (D) complex

3. The word “it” in the passage (in line 8, paragraph 1) refers to ________.

(A) human perception (B) light

(C) the natural world (D) a type of microscope

4. The author mentions the visible-light microscope in paragraph 1 in order to ________.

(A) put the X-ray microscope in a historical perspective

(B) begin a discussion of sixteenth century discoveries

(C) show how limited its uses are

(D) explain how it functioned

5. Why did it take so long to develop the X-ray microscope?

(A) Funds for research were insufficient.

(B) Materials used to manufacture X-ray tubes were difficult to obtain.

(C) The source of illumination was not bright enough until recently.

(D) X-ray microscopes were too complicated to operate.

6. Which of the following best expresses the essential information in the highlighted sentence (in paragraph 2)? *Incorrect* answer choices change the meaning in important ways or leave out essential information.
   (A) The development of the X-ray microscope slowed so that the development of the electron microscope progressed rapidly.
   (B) The development of the X-ray microscope stopped because of the rapid progress of the electron microscope.
   (C) The development of the electron microscope contributed to the development of the X-ray microscope.
   (D) The rapid progress of the electron microscope was attributed to the halted development of the X-ray microscope.

7. The word "considerably" in the passage (in line 1, paragraph 3) is closest in meaning to ________.
   (A) equally (B) quite (C) respectably (D) tolerably

8. The word "Rather" in the passage (in line 10, paragraph 3) is closest in meaning to ________.
   (A) Somewhat (B) Preferably
   (C) Instead (D) Significantly

9. The word "those" in the passage (in line 11, paragraph 3) refers to ________.
   (A) properties (B) microscopes
   (C) investigations (D) X-rays

10. Based on the information in the passage, what can be inferred about X-ray microscopes in the future?
   (A) They will probably replace electron microscopes altogether.
   (B) The will eventually be much cheaper to produce than they are now.
   (C) The will eventually change the illumination range that they now use.
   (D) They will provide information not available from other kinds of microscopes.

Source：雲科大 99 學年度碩士班招生考試試題

解答

1. (B) discover single-celled plants and animals they had never seen before
2. (C) tiny 極小的；微小的（minuscule）
3. (D) a type of microscope
4. (A) put the X-ray microscope in a historical perspective
5. (C) The source of illumination was not bright enough until recently.
6. (B) The development of the X-ray microscope stopped because of the rapid progress of the electron microscope.
7. (B) quite 相當；頗（considerably）
8. (C) Instead 反而；卻（Rather）
9. (C) investigations (those)
10. (D) They will provide information not available from other kinds of microscopes.

- **Introduction（引言段）：**

  Thesis Statement：Each advance in microscopic technique has provided scientists with new perspectives on the function of living organisms and the nature of matter itself.（顯微鏡技術的每一個進步，曾提供給科學家們新的觀點，以觀察活的有機體與物質本質）。

- **第二段：**

  主題句：The dream of building an X-ray microscope dates to 1895.

  中心思想（關鍵字）：X-ray microscope。

  闡述句策略：中間掃描時間法（1895, 1940's）；對比法（however）；因果法（As a result）。

  結論句：As a result, the brightness available today is millions of times that of X-ray tubes, which, for most of the century, were the only available sources of soft X-ray.

- **第三段：**

  主題句：The new X-ray microscopes **considerably** improve on the resolution provided by optical microscopes.

  中心思想（關鍵字）：new X-ray microscopes。

  闡述句策略：中間掃描對比法（Unlike conventional electron microscopy, ...）。

  結論句：**Rather**, their special properties will make possible investigations that will complement **those** performed with light - and electron - based instruments.

- **Conclusion（結論段）：**N / A。

各類公職考試閱讀測驗

A

Educational researchers have identified four distinctive learning styles used by students who are attempting to master new information and concepts. First, some students prefer __32__ learning. They learn best form lectures, tapes recordings, and class discussions. The second of these styles is __33__ learning. This is a learning-by-doing approach, which __34__ such things as dissecting animals to handle their internal organs rather than reading about them. Still other students are best __35__ to experiential learning. Making use of all their senses, such as a field trip to a forest when studying botany, is the best way for these learners to understand new material fully. The last of these styles is visual learning. The student who favors this style relies heavily on what can be seen—books and charts, __36__ —to acquire knowledge. Of these four learning styles, none is considered best; but rather they are descriptive of techniques individuals use to learn effectively.

32. (A) olfactory (B) auditory
    (C) visionary (D) imaginary
33. (A) tacit (B) tactical
    (C) taciturn (D) tactile
34. (A) imposes (B) explains
    (C) involves (D) excludes
35. (A) suited (B) admitted
    (C) attributed (D) ascribed

36. (A) in vain (B) after all
(C) by chance (D) for instance

Source：101 年公務人員特種考試，外交領事人員外交行政人員考試試題

解答

32. (B) auditory 聽覺的

33. (D) tactile 觸覺的

34. (C) involves 包含

35. (A) suited 適合的

36. (D) for instance 例如

- **主題句：** Educational researchers have identified four distinctive learning styles used by students who are attempting to master new information and concepts.
- **中心思想（關鍵字）：** four learning styles。
- **闡述句策略：** 分類法（First, second, Still other students, the last of these styles）。
- **結論句：** Of these four learning styles, none is considered best; but rather they are descriptive of techniques individuals use to learn effectively.
- **大意：** 教育研究人員已經辨識出四種不同的學習風格，學生們以資用來嘗試掌握新資訊與概念。接著作者以分類法分別說明四種不同的學習風格。

B

In January 2000, a Japanese government commission published a report that outlined the main goals for Japan in the twenty-first century. In the face of economic recession, rising crime rates and high unemployment, the commission was set up by the prime minister and given the task of __24__ a new course for the country in the coming decades. The commission's main findings surprised many people: Japanese citizens need to loosen their hold on some of their core values if the country is to address its current social ills successfully. The commission concluded that Japanese culture places too much value on conformity and equality, and called for action to reduce the "excessive degree of __25__ and uniformity" in society. It pointed to some basic facets of Japanese life which __26__ this conformity: almost all schoolchildren in Japan wear identical dark-blue uniforms that mask signs of individuality, while employees generally stay late at the office __27__ they do not need to because of an unspoken rule about leaving early. These values, the commission concluded, prevented Japanese people from __28__ notions of individual empowerment that would be essential in the coming years.

24. (A) charting (B) denouncing (C) boycotting (D) hampering
25. (A) variation (B) idiosyncrasy (C) homogeneity (D) segregation
26. (A) distract (B) reflect (C) transform (D) exaggerate

27. (A) only when (B) even if
    (C) because (D) if
28. (A) abolishing (B) marginalizing
    (C) weakening (D) embracing

Source：100 年公務人員特種考試，民航人員、外交領事人員及國際新聞人員考試試題

解答

24. (A) charting（詳細計畫）
25. (C) homogeneity（同質性）
26. (B) reflect（反映）
27. (B) even if（即使）
28. (D) embracing（擁抱）

- **主題句：** In January 2000, a Japanese government commission published a report that outlined the main goals for Japan in the twenty-first century.
- **中心思想（關鍵字）：** report, man goals。
- **闡述句策略：** 因果法（In the face of economic recession, rising crime rates and high unemployment）；例證法（Japanese citizens need to loosen their hold on some of their core values）。
- **結論句：** These values, the commission concluded, prevented Japanese people from ___28___ notions of individual empowerment that would be essential in the coming years.

- **大意：**2000 年 1 月時，一個日本政府委員會出版了一份報告，概要列出 21 世紀日本的主要目標。

C

Every culture prescribes certain occasions and ceremonies for giving gifts, whether for personal or professional reasons. Japanese gift-giving rituals show how tremendously important these acts are in that culture, where the wrapping of a gift is as important (if not more so) than the gift itself. The economic value of a gift is __36__ to its symbolic meaning. To the Japanese, gifts are viewed as an important aspect of one's duty to others in one's social group. Giving is a moral __37__ (known as giri). Highly ritualized gift-giving occurs during the giving of both household / personal gifts and company / professional gifts. Each Japanese has a well-defined set of relatives and friends with which he or she shares __38__ gift-giving obligations (kosai). **Personal gifts** are given on social occasions, such as at funerals, to people who are hospitalized, to mark __39__ from one life stage to another (e.g., weddings, birthdays), and as greetings (e.g., when one meets a visitor). **Company gifts** are given to commemorate the anniversary of a corporation's founding, the opening of a new building, or when new products are announced. In keeping with the Japanese emphasis on __40__, presents are not opened in front of the giver so that it will not be necessary to hide one's possible disappointment with the present.

36. (A) legendary (B) primary (C) secondary (D) satisfactory

37. (A) victory (B) dilemma
    (C) imperative (D) encouragement
38. (A) intentional (B) financial
    (C) overwhelming (D) reciprocal
39. (A) movements (B) assignments
    (C) compliments (D) establishments
40. (A) earning money (B) keeping time
    (C) saving face (D) showing pride

Source：99 年公務人員特種考試，外交領事人員及國際新聞人員考試試題

解答

36. (C) secondary 次要的

37. (C) imperative 必須履行的責任

38. (D) reciprocal 相互的；互惠的

39. (A) movements 移動；變動

40. (C) saving face 維護（保留）面子

- **主題句：**Every culture prescribes certain occasions and ceremonies for giving gifts, whether for personal or professional reasons.
- **中心思想（關鍵字）：**occasions and ceremonies for giving gifts。
- **闡述句策略：**例證法（Japanese gift-giving rituals, such as）；分類法（personal gifts, company gifts）。
- **結論句：**N / A。

- **大意：**無論是由於個人或職業上的原因，對於給禮品的時機與儀式，每一個文化都有規定。

D

If a successful longevity treatment were to emerge suddenly out of all the new developments of medical science, tacking on extra decades or even centuries to our lives, the results could be disastrous. It might very well be a case of the cure's being **worse than** the disease. This would be true even for the individuals lucky enough to receive the treatment. Presumably any treatment that conferred long life would keep people generally healthy, **but** the extra years would be a kind of medical balancing act, akin to the jugglers who dash about keeping plates spinning on top of poles. It would be **nerve-racking** at best.

What if the treatments did little or nothing to help one's memory? This is a crucial point that is often **overlooked** in discussions of longevity. The brain is by far the most complex organ known to us, and the workings of memory **are not really understood**. Keeping the body alive might be possible before we could do anything to strengthen or restore lost memories. Even the ordinary lifetime often seems too much for human memory to hold or recall, and if decades were tacked on, the long middle years of a life might be substantially **forgotten**, leaving only dim memories of childhood and recent events. If that were the case, the whole point of the exercise would be **lost**, for it is memory that makes us human.

32. What is the main concern of this passage?
    (A) Ways to prolong human's life in the future.
    (B) The importance of longevity in human life.
    (C) The possible problems people might face when life is prolonged.
    (D) The difficulties of prolonging human life at the present time.

33. According to the passage, which of the following statements is true?
    (A) Brain's function is the result of medical balance.
    (B) Brain's function is not well understood by scientists now.
    (C) Human brain is a nerve-racking system.
    (D) Brain's function is easily overlooked.

34. According to the passage, what makes us human?
    (A) Our body
    (B) Our nerve system
    (C)Our health
    (D) Our memory

35. According to the passage, lengthening one's life successfully might be .
    (A) catastrophic
    (B) rewarding
    (C) exciting
    (D) impressive

36. According to the passage, the sentence "It might very well be the case of the cure's being worse than the disease" implies that.
    (A) living a short life is worse than leading a long life

(B) no medicine can cure this disease

(C) it is impossible to balance the medical treatment

(D) the result of longevity might not be welcomed

Source：98 年公務人員特種考試，外交領事人員及國際新聞人員考試試題

解答

32. (C) The possible problems people might face when life is prolonged.

33. (B) Brain's function is not well understood by scientists now.
(The brain is by far the most complex organ known to us, and the workings of memory **are not really understood.**)

34. (D) Our memory (If that were the case, the whole point of the exercise would be **lost**, for it is memory that makes us human.)

35. (A) catastrophic (the results could be disastrous.)

36. (D) the result of longevity might not be welcomed

- **主題句：**If a successful longevity treatment were to emerge suddenly out of all the new developments of medical science, tacking on extra decades or even centuries to our lives, the results could be disastrous.
- **中心思想（關鍵字）：**the results could be disastrous。
- **闡述句策略：**描述問題法（worse than, but, nerve-racking, overlooked, not understood, forgotton, lost）。
- **結論句：**If that were the case, the whole point of the exercise would be lost, for it is memory that makes us human.

- **大意：**如果從新的醫學發展中，突然出現一種成功的長壽治療方法，在我們生命加上另外數十年或甚至幾世紀，這樣的結果可能是大災難。

E

For centuries, explorers have risked their lives venturing into the unknown for reasons that were to varying degrees economic and nationalistic. Christopher Columbus went west to look for better trade routes to the Orient and to promote the greater glory of Spain. Lewis and Clark journeyed into the American wilderness to find out what the U.S. had acquired in the Louisiana Purchase, and the Apollo astronauts rocketed to the moon in a dramatic flexing of technological muscle during the cold war.

Although their missions blended commercial and political-military **imperatives**, the explorers involved all accomplished some significant science simply by going where no scientists had gone before. The Lewis and Clark team brought back samples, descriptions and drawings of the flora and fauna of the western U.S., much of it new to the colonizers and the culture they represented. The Apollo program, too, eventually gushed good data. "Our fundamental understanding of the overall geological history of the moon is largely derived from the last three Apollo missions," says Paul D. Spudis, a geologist and staff scientist at the Lunar and Planetary Institute in Houston.

Today Mars looms as humanity's next great terra incognita. And with dubious prospects for a short-term financial return, and amid a growing emphasis on international cooperation in large space ventures, it is clear that imperatives other than profits or nationalism will have to compel human beings to leave their tracks on the planet's ruddy surface.

33. The word **imperatives** in the second paragraph most likely means.
    (A) commands (B) astronauts
    (C) reasons (D)voyages

34. What is the main idea of this passage?
    (A) Mars will be the next place humans will explore.
    (B) People explore for a mixture of economic and nationalistic reasons.
    (C) Lewis and Clark brought back important information about the American west.
    (D) Columbus wanted to get to the East by sailing west.

35. The author's purpose in discussing the exploration of the moon and the American west is to ________.
    (A) persuade the reader to pay tribute to famous explorers
    (B) inform the reader about history
    (C) hint at reasons for future missions to Mars
    (D) narrate an interesting series of events

Source：95 年公務人員特種考試，外交領事人員及國際新聞人員考試試題

解答

33. (C) reasons (imperatives)

34. (B) People explore for a mixture of economic and nationalistic reasons.
(...explorers have risked their lives venturing into the unknown for reasons that were to varying degrees economic and nationalistic.)

35. (C) hint at reasons for future missions to Mars
(Today Mars looms as humanity's next great terra incognita.)

- **Introduction（引言段）：**

Thesis Statement：For centuries, explorers have risked their lives venturing into the unknown for reasons that were to varying degrees economic and nationalistic.（好幾個世紀以來，探險家曾經冒著生命危險進入未知的地方，為了不同程度的經濟的與國家主義的原因）。

- **第二段：**

主題句：Although their missions blended commercial and political-military **imperatives**, the explorers involved all accomplished some significant science simply by going where no scientists had gone before.

中心思想（關鍵字）：accomplished some significant science。

闡述句策略：中間掃描例證法（the Lewis and Clark team, Apollo program）。

結論句：N / A。

- **Conclusion（結論段）：**

Thesis statement：...,it is clear that imperatives other than profits or nationalism will have to compel human beings to leave their tracks on the planet's ruddy surface.（很清楚的，除了利潤或國家主義以外，還有其他的原因將強迫人類在行星紅色的表面上留下足跡）。

F

Let's picture a huge public gathering - like the hajj to Mecca. Think of the World Cup, the Olympics, or a rock concert. When thousands or even millions of people get together, what will be the biggest health concern? Traditionally, doctors and public health officials were most concerned about the spread of infectious diseases. Robert Steffen, a professor of travel medicine at the University of Zurich, says that infectious diseases are still a concern, but injuries are a bigger threat at so-called mass gatherings.

According to Professor Steffen, children and older people have the highest risk of injury or other health problems at mass gathering events. Children are at more risk of getting crushed in stampedes, while older people are at higher risk of heat stroke and dying from extreme heat.

Stampedes at mass gatherings have caused an estimated seven thousand deaths over the past thirty years. The design of an area for mass gathering can play a part. There may be narrow passages or other choke points that too many people try to use at once. The mood of a crowd can also play a part. Organizers of large gatherings need to avoid creating conditions that might lead to stampedes and heat stroke.

So what advice does Professor Steffen have for people attending a large gathering? First, get needed vaccinations before traveling. Then, stay away from any large mass of people as much as possible. Also, be careful with alcohol and drugs, which can increase the risk of injuries.

71. Which of the following would be the most appropriate title for this passage?
    (A) How to avoid mass gatherings
    (B) Mass gathering: New escape skills
    (C) Infectious diseases: New cures found
    (D) Health risks in a crowd: Not what you may think

72. Which of the following is closest in meaning to **stampede** in the passage?
    (A) A plane crash
    (B) A steamy factory
    (C) A sudden rush of a crowd
    (D) Heat stroke due to mass gathering events

73. According to Professor Steffen, which of the following is more threatening to the health of people attending a huge public gathering?
    (A) Injuries
    (B) Infectious diseases
    (C) The mood of event organizers
    (D) Insufficient budget for an event

74. Which of the following is clear from the passage?
    (A) Infectious disease is no longer a concern of the public.
    (B) Event organizers should be more careful to avoid stampedes.

(C) A proper place for mass gathering should have one narrow passage.
(D) Children and older people are prohibited to attend mass gatherings.

75. Which of the following statements is LEAST supported in the passage?
(A) Extreme heat can cause death at mass gatherings.
(B) Infectious diseases will not spread at mass gatherings.
(C) Alcohol can increase the risk of injuries at mass gatherings.
(D) Older people are likely to suffer from heat stroke at a large gathering.

Source：101 年專門職業及技術人員普通考試，導遊人員、領隊人員考試試題

解答

71. (D) Health risks in a crowd: Not what you may think
(but injuries are a bigger threat at so-called mass gatherings.)

72. (C) A sudden rush of a crowd
(Children are at more risk of getting crushed in stampedes,...)

73. (A) Injuries
(but injuries are a bigger threat at so-called mass gatherings.)

74. (B) Event organizers should be more careful to avoid stampedes.
(Organizers of large gatherings need to avoid creating conditions that might lead to stampedes and heat stroke.)

75. (B) Infectious diseases will not spread at mass gatherings.

- **Introduction（引言段）：**

  Thesis Statement：but injuries are a bigger threat at so-called mass gatherings.（在所謂的大型集會，傷害是更大的威脅）。

- **第二段：**

  主題句：According to Professor Steffen, children and older people have the highest risk of injury or other health problems at mass gathering events.

  中心思想（關鍵字）：risk of injury or other health problems。

  闡述句策略：中間掃描因果法（caused, play a part）。

  結論句：Organizers of large gatherings need to avoid creating conditions that might lead to stampedes and heat stroke.

- **Conclusion（結論段）：**

  Thesis statement：So what advice does Professor Steffen have for people attending a large gathering? (First, Second, Also).（所以對於人們參加大型集會，Steffen教授提供什麼忠告呢？〔第一，第二，另外〕）。

G

While on vacation, not everyone likes staying at nice hotels, visiting museums, and shopping at department stores. Some would rather jump out of an airplane, speed down a river, or stay in a traditional village. They are part of a growing number of people who enjoy adventure tourism. It is a type of travel for people looking to get more out of their vacations.

With the Internet, it is easier than ever to set up an adventure tour. People can plan trips themselves, or they can find a suitable tour company online. Some popular countries to visit are Costa Rica, India, New Zealand, and Botswana. Their natural settings make them perfect for outdoor activities like hiking and diving. **Rich** in wildlife, they are also great for bird watching and safaris. Learning about the local history and culture is also popular with adventure travelers. In Peru, people love visiting the ruins of Machu Picchu. And, travelers in Tanzania enjoy meeting local tribes. In some countries, it is even possible to live and work in a village during a vacation. While building houses and helping research teams, travelers can enjoy local food and learn about the culture.

Besides being a lot of fun, these exiting trips mean big money for local economies. Tourism is already the world's largest industry, worth some $ 3 trillion. Of that, adventure tourism makes up about 20% of the market. That number is growing, as more people plan exciting vacations in their own countries and abroad.

76. What can we infer about adventure tourists from the passage?
    (A) They like safe and comfortable vacations.
    (B) They have little interest in culture.
    (C) They enjoy trips that are exciting.
    (D) They rarely play on sports teams.

77. Where would you go to visit Machu Picchu?
    (A) Tanzania (B) Europe
    (C) Peru (D) The Himalayas

78. What is **NOT** a reason why people enjoy traveling to New Zealand?
    (A) Tours there are cheaper than in other places.
    (B) It is a great place for nature lovers.
    (C) One could easily set up a bird watching trip.
    (D) There are many outdoor activities.

79. What does the word **rich** in paragraph 2 mean?
    (A) wealthy (B) plentiful (C) funny (D) heavy

80. What does the passage suggest about the tourism industry?
    (A) It may soon be worth $3 trillion.
    (B) Adventure tourism brings in the most money.
    (C) Most of the industry is facing hard times.
    (D) It is important to local economies.

Source：99年專門職業及技術人員普通考試，導遊人員、領隊人員考試試題

解答

76. (C) They enjoy trips that are exciting.
    (Besides being a lot of fun, these exiting trips mean big money for local economies.)

77. (C) Peru (In Peru, people love visiting the ruins of Machu Picchu.)

78. (A) Tours there are cheaper than in other places.

79. (B) plentiful（豐富的；充足的；多的）（rich in 富於……的；有很多……的）

80. (D) It is important to local economies.
    (Besides being a lot of fun, these exiting trips mean big money for local economies.)

- **Introduction（引言段）：**

  Thesis Statement： They are part of a growing number of people who enjoy adventure tourism.（有愈來愈多喜歡冒險觀光的人，他們是一部分）。

- **第二段：**

  主題句： With the Internet, it is easier than ever to set up an adventure tour.

  中心思想（關鍵字）： adventure tour。

  闡述句策略： 中間掃描例證法（Costa Rica, India, New Zealand, and Botswana, in Peru）。

  結論句： N / A。

- **Conclusion（結論段）：**

  Thesis statement： That number is growing, as more people plan exciting vacations in their own countries and abroad.（因為更多人計畫在他們自己國家與國外度刺激的假期，所以那個數字正在成長）。

H

A tour manager has individual duties to perform to run a tour smoothly and successfully. For instance, the tour manager should always be the first one up every morning in order to make sure each team member is ready before the bus leaves for the next scenic spot each day.

The tour manager will also check for possible changes to the itinerary. Most days of a tour require a long bus trip to the next **venue**. The traveling time may be the only opportunity for the tour manager to undertake much of the administrative chores: paper work, phone calls, and planning for the next few days. This may include confirming and reconfirming hotel reservations, return flights, and arrival time at restaurants and scenic spots.

It usually falls to the tour manager to keep the team members and the service crew happy while they are hundreds, or thousands, of miles away from their homes and their families. The tour manager shall keep everyone working as a team and deal with individual problems, such as stolen passports, physical ailments and medical emergencies. Most importantly, the tour manager must take the group members home safe and sound at the end of the journey and get ready for the next trip.

76. What is this passage mainly about?
   (A) Running a profitable tour.
   (B) Tips on booking cheap hotel rooms.
   (C) Enjoying tours.
   (D) The duties of a tour manager.

77. Which of the following is generally NOT considered a tour manager's responsibility?
   (A) Keep everyone happy. (B) Drive the tour bus.
   (C) Visit the resorts as scheduled. (D) Confirm hotel reservations.

78. Which of the following words is closest in meaning to the word "**venue**" in the passage?
   (A) Stand (B) Spot (C) Sport (D) Sigh

79. What will a responsible tour manager most likely do on the bus

during the tour?

(A) Make phone calls to friends.

(B) Buy discounted souvenirs for team members.

(C) Find seats with the best view for team members.

(D) Reconfirm return flights for team members.

80. What can be inferred from this passage?

(A) Most tours become mental and physical burdens for a tour manager.

(B) Most tours require tour members to pay extra fees for services.

(C) Most tour managers don't change their original itinerary.

(D) Most tour managers ask their group members to help with chores.

Source：98 年專門職業及技術人員普通考試，導遊人員、領隊人員考試試題

解答

76. (D) The duties of a tour manager.
(A tour manager has individual duties to perform to run a tour smoothly and successfully.)

77. (B) Drive the tour bus.

78. (B) Spot（venue 發生地；集合地）

79. (D) Reconfirm return flights for team members.
(This may include confirming and reconfirming hotel reservations, return flights, and arrival time at restaurants and scenic spots.)

80. (A) Most tours become mental and physical burdens for a tour manager.
(Most importantly, the tour manager must take the group members home safe and sound at the end of the journey and get ready for the next trip.)

- **Introduction（引言段）：**

Thesis Statement： A tour manager has individual duties to perform to run a tour smoothly and successfully.（旅遊經理有個別的職責要履行，須確保旅遊順利成功）。

- **第二段：**

主題句： The tour manager will also check for possible changes to the itinerary.

中心思想（關鍵字）： possible changes to the itinerary。

闡述句策略： 中間掃描例證法（paper work, phone calls, and planning for the next few days.）。

結論句： This may include confirming and reconfirming hotel reservations, return flights, and arrival time at restaurants and scenic spots.

- **Conclusion（結論段）：**

Thesis statement： Most importantly, the tour manager must take the group members home safe and sound at the end of the journey and get ready for the next trip.（最重要地，在旅行結束之時，旅遊經理必須將團員安然無恙地帶回家，並準備好下一個旅行）。

I

All over the world, one trendy, popular global diet is fast food-prepared items from inexpensive restaurants or snacks, food stands. Some examples of typically American fast food are hamburgers, hot dogs, sandwiches, fried chicken, and so on. For several reasons, many people choose fast food. First, it is quick and convenient. Second, it is cheaper than special home-cooked meals or formal restaurant dinners. And third, it is identical in every eating place with the same company name. The atmosphere and style of most fast-food places is casual, comfortable, and familiar. So why do other eaters dislike or stay away from this fast, easy kind of nourishment? The main reason is in its low nutritional value. Fast food does not contain large amounts of fiber, vitamins, minerals, and the like-elements necessary for good nutrition and health. In contrast, most types of fast food have a lot of fat, cholesterol, sugar, or salt in them. Possibly, these substances can cause or increase health disorders, like heart disease, strokes, and some kinds of cancer.

Some people believe food should be perfectly fresh and "natural". According to natural food eaters, fast food is not good for human beings. They do not believe convenience foodscanned, frozen, or packaged in other waysare very nutritious either. On the other hand, these quick and easy kinds of worldwide nourishment are generally getting better and more healthful. For instance, many fast-food restaurants now have salad bars and put vegetable items on their menus. In some places, customers can get fish or *veggieburgers* free of meat instead of hamburgers, and grilled chicken instead of fried. Also, some newer kinds of packaged and prepared foods contain less fat, cholesterol, sugar, or salt than before. Of course, people around the world like to **indulge** themselves with junk food, like candy, cookies, potato chips, ice cream, and other things without much nutritional value. For health and sales reasons, some snack food companies are producing packaged items with less fat, sugar, or salt. And nutrition barssnacks with a lot of protein, vitamins, and other nourishing food elementsare becoming more widely available.

71. What does paragraph 1 mainly discuss?
 (A) Some examples of typically American fast food.
 (B) The reasons why some people like fast food and others don't.
 (C) The substances that can be found in most types of fast food.
 (D) Some possible health disorders caused by fast food.

72. What does paragraph 2 mainly discuss?
 (A) Natural food eaters' views on fast food.
 (B) New items on fast-food restaurants' menus.
 (C) Recent improvements on fast food.
 (D) Newer kinds of packaged and prepared foods.

73. According to the passage, which of the following statements is true?
 (A) Home-made meals are in general cheaper than fast food.
 (B) Most people like eating natural food better than eating at fast-food restaurants.
 (C) Fast-food restaurants do not have salad bars or vegetable items.
 (D) Fast-food restaurants with the same name usually offer the same kinds of food.

74. According to the passage, which of the following is **NOT** one of the recent changes in the fast-food industry?
 (A) cutting down sales on hamburgers and snacks
 (B) providing salad bars and other vegetarian foods
 (C) cutting down sugar and salt in foods
 (D) providing low-fat and low-cholesterol foods

75. What does **indulge** in paragraph 2 mean?
(A) affect (B) enjoy (C) harm (D) warn

Source：97年專門職業及技術人員普通考試，導遊人員、領隊人員考試試題

解答

71. (B) The reasons why some people like fast food and others don't.
(For several reasons, many people choose fast food.
So why do other eaters dislike or stay away from this fast, easy kind of nourishment?)

72. (C) Recent improvements on fast food.
(On the other hand, these quick and easy kinds of worldwide nourishment are generally getting better and more healthful.)

73. (D) Fast-food restaurants with the same name usually offer the same kinds of food.
(Some examples of typically American fast food are hamburgers, hot dogs, sandwiches, fried chicken, and so on.)

74. (A) cutting down sales on hamburgers and snacks

75. (B) enjoy（indulge themselves with junk food，享受垃圾食物）

- **Introduction 段：**N / A。
- **第一段：**

主題句：For several reasons, many people choose fast food.
So why do other eaters dislike or stay away from this fast, easy kind of nourishment?

中心思想（關鍵字）：reasons。

闡述句策略：中間掃描因果法（First, Second, And third, the main reason）。

結論句：N / A。

- **第二段：**

主題句：On the other hand, these quick and easy kinds of worldwide nourishment are generally getting better and more healthful.

中心思想（關鍵字）：getting better and more healthful。

闡述句策略：中間掃描例證法（For example）。

結論句：

- **Conclusion 段：**N / A。

這是二段文章，無 Introduction 段與 Conclusion 段。

J

Tourism brings employment, investment and income to the Caribbean. People are employed directly in hotels, construction or government departments, but many more live indirectly from tourism as guides or taxi drivers. In total, the industry is the region's biggest employer. Yet the idyllic image of Caribbean tourism conceals many areas of conflict and controversy.

The older problems largely concern the disproportionate level of foreign control over the industry and the lack of local ownership and management. They also include perceptions among many islanders that tourism is a corrupting influence, linked to crime, prostitution and drug abuse. There is also concern that the creation of large tourist developments such as golf courses is having an adverse effect on the environment and wasting limited resources, not least water.

The growing popularity of cruise ships is another cause of criticism, as local hoteliers and restaurateurs are deprived of business by what are effectively floating resorts. The 1990s also witnessed the growth of "ecotourism" in more remote, unspoiled islands. More "up-market" higher-spending visitors were attracted there. However, fragile ecosystems and hitherto wild rainforests cannot absorb increasing numbers of nature-loving visitors.

76. The passage above is mainly about __________.
    (A) the history of Caribbean tourism
    (B) the benefits tourism brings to the region
    (C) the idyllic image of Caribbean tourism
    (D) the good and bad effects of Caribbean tourism

77. What kinds of people live on tourism indirectly?
    (A) tour guides and taxi drivers
    (B) farmers
    (C) factory workers
    (D) people hired by hotels

78. In what respect has Caribbean tourism been criticized for unfairness?
    (A) It wastes water.
    (B) The tourist industry is largely owned and managed by foreigners.
    (C) It creates golf courses, affecting the environment.
    (D) It destroys the idyllic image.

79. Why are cruise ships not welcomed by the locals?
    (A) They pollute the environment.
    (B) They are too popular.
    (C) They take away the business of the local hotels and restaurants.
    (D) They waste resources.

80. What is the main problem of "ecotourism"?
    (A) It only attracts "up-market" tourists.
    (B) It may damage the natural environment.
    (C) The islands concerned are remote and unspoiled.
    (D) The visitors concerned love nature too much.

Source：96 年專門職業及技術人員普通考試，導遊人員、領隊人員考試試題

解答

76. (D) the good and bad effects of Caribbean tourism
    (Yet the idyllic image of Caribbean tourism conceals many areas of conflict and controversy.)

77. (A) tour guides and taxi drivers
    (...but many more live indirectly from tourism as guides or taxi drivers.)

78. (B) The tourist industry is largely owned and managed by foreigners.
    (The older problems largely concern the disproportionate level of foreign control over the industry and the lack of local ownership and management.)

79. (C) They take away the business of the local hotels and restaurants.
    (as local hoteliers and restaurateurs are deprived of business by what are effectively floating resorts.)

解答

80. (B) It may damage the natural environment.
(The 1990s also witnessed the growth of "ecotourism" in more remote, unspoiled islands.)

- **Introduction（引言段）：**

Thesis Statement：Yet the idyllic image of Caribbean tourism conceals many areas of conflict and controversy.（然而加勒比海觀光田園詩的形象，隱藏許多方面的衝突與爭論）。

- **第二段：**

主題句：The older problems largely concern the disproportionate level of foreign control over the industry and the lack of local ownership and management.

中心思想（關鍵字）：

闡述句策略：中間掃描例證法（They also include perceptions, There is also concern）。

結論句：N / A。

- **第三段：**

主題句：The growing popularity of cruise ships is another cause of criticism, as local hoteliers and restaurateurs are deprived of business by what are effectively floating resorts.

中心思想（關鍵字）：

闡述句策略：中間掃描例證法（The 1990s also witnessed the growth of "ecotourism" in more remote, unspoiled islands.）。

結論句：N / A。

- **Conclusion（結論段）：**N / A。

【第五章】

□□□□□□

英文書本的閱讀策略

英文文章的閱讀策略

英文段落的閱讀策略

綜合練習

高層次的英文閱讀策略

做筆記的策略

前言

除了看懂英文以外，現代公民尚需具備高層次的閱讀與思考技能。讀者除了了解英文的字面意義以外，還需要提出自己的看法並說服其他人，換言之，無論讀者是同意或不同意該議題、支持或反對該議題、亦或持正面或負面的想法，均要言之有物，以具備口語與書面的表達能力。高層次的思考技能（higher-order / level thinking skills）有一些同義詞，譬如「批判式思考技能」（critical thinking skills）、「獨立思考技能」（independent thinking skills）、「分析式思考技能」（analytical thinking skills）等等。這種高層次的思考技能需以不同的閱讀方式來培養。

一般而言，英文閱讀策略分為三種：(1) bottom-up reading strategy（由下而上的閱讀策略）；(2) top-down reading strategy（由上而下的閱讀策略）；(3) interactive reading strategy（互動式的閱讀策略）。由下而上的閱讀策略，顧名思義就是由單字、片語、句型、文法的眼光去分析了解句子的意義，比較著重在局部的（local）分析，較為耗時，且會有見樹不見林的缺點。由上而下的閱讀策略是不從文法的眼光去分析了解句子的意義，比較著重在整體的（global）分析，了解文章的大意與組織方式，因此較有效率。而互動式的閱讀策略，就是讀者與文本互動，作者將思想化為文字，而讀者透過閱讀的過程，將文字轉換成思想。

許多專家學者大力推廣閱讀素養的重要性，而臺灣的學生在「國際閱讀素養發展研究」（PIRLS - Progress in International Reading Literacy Study）與「國際學生評量計畫」（PISA - Program for International Student Assessment）兩項閱讀評比中，表現低落。這凸顯出臺灣的學生在詮釋（interpretation）、整合（synthesis）、檢驗（verification）、評估（evaluation）文章意義的高層次思考能力方面，有偏弱的現象。因此，我們應致力於高層次的閱讀策略，以幫助學生提升思考力。

高層次的閱讀策略有很多，本書先介紹以下的幾種：(1) Benjamin Bloom's Educational Taxonomy 布魯姆教育分類法、(2) Reciprocal Teaching 相互教學法、(3) Questioning the Author 提問作者法、(4) SWOT Analysis SWOT 分析法、(5) Topical Structure Analysis（TSA）主題結構分析。

高層次的英文閱讀策略

一、Benjamin Bloom's Educational Taxonomy

一般的問題分為二種：封閉式問題與開放式問題。封閉式問題（closed-ended questions）通常會限制回答者從表列的答案中選擇回答，這些問題通常是以是非題或選擇題的方式呈現。而開放式問題（open-ended questions）與封閉式問題相反，通常是以敘述的問題方式呈現，要求回答者回應，例如「你為什麼選擇那個答案」？

高層次的思考技巧有別於封閉式問題的回覆方式，而是一種能夠回覆較深層問題（例如開放式問題）的思考技巧。譬如托福寫作測驗（Test of Written English，簡稱 TWE），論文寫作中是用到「解釋」與「說服」的技巧，考生需運用個人的知識與經驗敘述、表達自己的意見或主張、解釋原因，以支持自己的想法與說服讀者，這類考題即是測驗考生較高層次的思考能力，例如，要考生闡述「Some people prefer to work for a large company. Others prefer to work for a small company. Which would you prefer? Please provide specific reasons and / or examples to support your position.」。又例如，要學生闡述「Why did the Second World War break out?」這類說明事件發生原因的考題，其問題的深度層次明顯高於要學生寫出事件發生的年代與參戰的國家。

為培養讀者多學習思考內容的深度及事件發生所代表的意義，而不只是死背學習的內容，我們應該多利用 Bloom 所提的「教育分類法」中，Analysis 層次以上的「問題提示」來培育自己高層次的思考技能，例如：運用 analyze / What if ? / summarize / assess / create 等「問題提示」來詢問自己，從文中找出答案，如此一來高層次思考能力的提升便指日可待。

Bloom's Taxonomy（1956）教育分類法，雖已經過數十年，仍被學者廣泛討論與應用，對我們仍極富參考價值。他創造此教育分類法，將教育場景當中時常出現的問題種類按照層次加以分類，思考能力可歸納成六大分類，這個分類法提供了一個很有用的架構，讀者可根據問題提示（question cues）而判斷其所屬的問題層次，而運用合適的策略加以因應。

然而讀者需注意兩點：第一點，Bloom 當年所謂的 Knowledge 層次定義，不同於今日 Knowledge is power 的定義，當初的 Knowledge 應屬記憶層次。第二點，最高層次 Evaluation 已修改為 Creativity（創造或創新）層次，比較符合現代教育所需。編者根據其分類層次由上而下，列舉出每大類的定義與幾個「問題提示」如下表，協助讀者理解與熟悉其意義並有效運用。

Educational Taxonomy：Competence（教育分類法：能力）	Definition（定義） / Question Cues（問題提示）	
Evaluation（評估） / Creativity（創造）	定義	1. 比較與區別想法（compare and discriminate ideas） 2. 評估理論與報告的價值（assess value of theories, presentations）

		3. 根據論點作選擇（make choices based on reasoned argument） 4. 核對證據的價值（verify value of evidence） 5. 識別主觀性（recognize subjectivity） 6. 創新（creative or innovate）
	問題提示	assess, decide, rank, grade, test, measure, recommend, convince, select, judge, explain, discriminate, support, conclude, compare, summarize, create, innovate
Synthesis（綜合）	定義	1. 使用舊想法以創造新想法（use old ideas to create new ones） 2. 從既有事實推斷（generalize from given facts） 3. 從好幾個領域使知識相聯繫（relate knowledge from several areas） 4. 預測、做出結論（predict, draw conclusions）
	問題提示	combine, integrate, modify, rearrange, substitute, plan, create, design, invent, what if?, compose, formulate, prepare, generalize, rewrite
Analysis（分析）	定義	1. 看出樣式（seeing patterns） 2. 部分的組織（organization of parts） 3. 認識隱藏的意義（recognition of hidden meanings） 4. 辨識構成要素（identification of components）
	問題提示	analyze, separate, order, explain, connect, classify, arrange, divide, compare, select, explain, infer
Application（應用）	定義	1. 使用資訊（use information） 2. 使用方法、概念、理論於新的情境中（use methods, concepts, theories in new situations）

<table>
<tr><td rowspan="2"></td><td></td><td>3. 使用習得的技能或知識來解決問題（solve problems using required skills or knowledge）</td></tr>
<tr><td>問題提示</td><td>apply, demonstrate, calculate, complete, illustrate, show, solve, examine, modify, relate, change, classify, experiment, discover</td></tr>
<tr><td rowspan="2">Comprehension
（理解）</td><td>定義</td><td>1. 了解資訊（understanding information）
2. 掌握意義（grasp meaning）
3. 將知識轉換成新的背景（translate knowledge into new context）
4. 詮釋事實、比較、對比（interpret facts, compare, contrast）
5. 列順序、分類、推論原因（order, group, infer causes）
6. 預測結果（predict consequences）</td></tr>
<tr><td>問題提示</td><td>summarize, describe, interpret, contrast, predict, associate, distinguish, estimate, differentiate, discuss, extend</td></tr>
<tr><td rowspan="2">Knowledge
（知識）</td><td>定義</td><td>1. 觀察與資訊的記憶（observation and recall of information）
2. 日期、事件、地點的知識（knowledge of dates, events, places）
3. 大意的知識（knowledge of major ideas）
4. 熟練某題材（mastery of subject matter）</td></tr>
<tr><td>問題提示</td><td>list, define, tell, describe, identify, show, label, collect, examine, tabulate, quote, name, who, when, where, etc.</td></tr>
</table>

Adapted from Bloom's Educational Taxonomy (1956).

二、Reciprocal Teaching: Predicting, Questioning, Clarifying, Summarizing (PQCS)

相互教學法包括預測（predicting）、提問（questioning）、澄清（clarifying）與摘要（summarizing），可以上述的順序進行閱讀，也可改變以上的順序進行閱讀。若是一班的英文閱讀課，可以分組的方式（三至五人一組）進行此法。以下的施作方式並非一成不變，師生可彈性調整運用。

PQCS 表

Predicting（預測）
學生們使用預測的方式以準備閱讀。組長從文章標題預測第一段，第一段看完預測第二段，依此類推。組員建議修改或增加預測。 程序： 1. 學生將預測的內容以口頭或書面的方式呈現給全班。 2. 正確的預測內容予以稱讚。 3. 不正確的預測內容予以討論。 4. 各組互相觀摩學習或挑戰彼此之預測內容。
Questioning（提問）
讀完文章後，各組組長向其組員提問，以確定組員了解文章大意與內容。 程序： 1. 組長問組員文章作者的立場（position, stance, perspective, opinion）。 2. 組長問組員文章各段大意（topic sentence, main idea）。 3. 組長問組員文章各段內容（supporting sentences 的技巧）。 4. 組長問組員文章結論段（最後一段）中作者的立場。
Clarifying（澄清）
組長指出文章中有困惑與較困難理解的地方，組員也指出文章中有困惑與較困難理解的部分。然後整組討論這些有問題的內容，再從文章當中找資訊以解決這些問題與澄清疑惑。

程序：
1. 組長指出文章中有困惑與較困難理解的部分，討論與澄清三至五個問題。
2. 組員指出文章中有困惑與較困難理解的部分，討論與澄清三至五個問題。
3. 整組討論這些有問題的部分，然後從文章當中找資訊以解決這些問題與澄清疑惑。
4. 教師可指定段落，或由各組組長或組員決定澄清的段落或有問題的部分。

Summarizing（摘要）
各組組長將文章摘要，組員建議增加或修改摘要，接著組長評估組員的回應，最後教師評估與回饋。
程序：
1. 組長選擇一組員擔任秘書（secretary），將摘要寫下。
2. 組長選擇另一組員擔任偵探（detective），找文章證據支持或反對摘要內容。
3. 組長選擇另一組員擔任評論員（commentator）以分析摘要。
4. 教師評估與回饋各組。

三、Questioning the Author

以下表格為提問作者參考項目，師生可以討論增加或修改內容，以符合教學場景需要。

Questioning the Author: Generalized questions

1. What difficulties am I having in understanding the text?
   （在了解文章內容時，我遇到什麼困難？）
2. What are the main ideas in the text?
   （文章的大意是什麼？）
3. Why does the author say what she or he does?
   （為什麼作者說她或他所做的事情？）

4. Does the author explain this clearly?
(作者有清楚地解釋這個嗎？)
5. How could the author say this more clearly?
(作者可以如何說，而更清楚？)
6. How does this fit with what the author has already said?
(這個與作者先前所說的有符合嗎？)
7. What types of examples should have been added?
(應該再增加何種例子？)
8. How does the author signal main ideas (and how well)?
(作者如何標示大意？)
9. Did the author give us the answer to the issue that she or he has raised?
(作者所提出的問題，有沒有給我們答案？)
10. What biases or perspectives does the author reveal?
(作者有顯示偏見或觀點嗎？)
11. What is the significance of the author's message?
(作者訊息的重要性為何？)
12. How does the information presented here connect to what we have read before?
(這裡所提出的資訊，與我們之前讀過的內容有何關連？)
13. How effectively are the ideas presented?
(所提出的想法，有無給人深刻印象？)
14. What is the usefulness of the text information?
(文章資訊有何用處？)

Adapted from *Reading in a second language: Moving from theory to practice*, William Grabe, Cambridge University Press, NY: New York (2009, p. 236).

四、SWOT Analysis

此策略分析法是由 Albert Humphreym 所提出來的。他於 1960 與 1970 年代使用美國 Fortune 500 公司的資料所提出的策略，是一種企業競爭態勢分析方法，通過評估企業的優勢（Strengths）、劣勢（Weaknesses）、競爭市場上的機會（Opportunities）和威脅（Threats），用以在制定企業的發展策略前，對企業進行深入的全面分析以及競爭優勢的定位。其中優勢與劣勢是內在因素（internal factors），而機會和威脅是外在環境因素（external factors）。此方法後來被廣泛使用在各個領域，雖然有時被批評為過度使用或濫用，但仍有其引用價值。

編者在大學任教時，常鼓勵學生善用此方法，成效良好。SWOT 分析通常以表格的方式呈現，而英文閱讀策略的運用可以表述如下：

Strengths：（本文的優點） 1. 2. 3.	Weaknesses：（本文的缺點） 1. 2. 3.
Opportunities：（本文與外在環境的機會）—建議可使用假設句（If / 如果……） 1. 2. 3.	Threats / Challenges：（本文與外在環境的威脅或挑戰）—建議可使用假設句（If / 如果……） 1. 2. 3.
Remarks:	

以下提供一範例供讀者參考

<table>
<tr><td>Strengths：（優點）
1. 是目前少數將管理控制制度與策略形態一起做研究，可了解什麼樣的策略形態是採用何種管理控制。
2. 明確地指出過去學者在管理控制制度上的各種研究結果。
3. 本文也將各種經典的策略形態都整合在一起，也引述諸多策略大師的學術貢獻。</td><td>Weaknesses：（缺點）
1. 過於單純談論各策略形態所採用的管理控制制度，而未考量到組織文化的不同是否也會影響控制形態。
2. 未將一些環境因素放入研究做比較（如法規、科技、規模、資本、經濟大環境等因素）。</td></tr>
<tr><td>Opportunities：（機會）
1. 可探討管理控制制度在環境因素、策略導向、科技導向對經營績效之間運作的影響。
2. 可針對管理控制是否會因為組織文化的不同而影響經營績效。</td><td>Threats / Challenges：（威脅或挑戰）
1. 已經有愈來愈多的學者在實務面探討管理控制對企業績效的影響，若只單一在理論面去做研究，可能會產生實務與理論無法契合的情形，而目前愈來愈多的研究都針對管理控制制度來提出最新論。</td></tr>
<tr><td colspan="2">Remarks:</td></tr>
</table>

SWOT 範例（企管碩士班期末報告）

針對 British Journal of Management Vol. 11, 197-212（2000）的文章 On Strategy and Management Control: The Importance of Classifying the Strategy of the Business.

五、Topical Structure Analysis (TSA)

主題結構分析可以用來分析文章的一致性或連貫性（coherence）。芬蘭的語言學家將文章的行進方式分為 parallel progression（平行的行進方式）、sequential progression（順序的行進方式）、extended parallel progression（延伸的平行行進方式）。

主題分析的四個步驟：

1. 文章或段落中的每一個句子標出數字。
2. 標明每句中的主題（單字或片語）
3. 畫出段落句子的圖形。
4. 檢查句子之間想法的連貫性，並酌予修改。

範例1 **Parallel progression：the themes are semantically co-referential**（主題在語意上指涉相同）

Example:

(1) **Clinical depression** is not a sign of personal weakness, or a condition that can be willed away. (2) In fact, **it** often interferes with a person's ability or will to get help. (3) **It** is a serious illness that lasts for weeks, months and sometimes years. (4) **It** may even influence someone to contemplate or attempt suicide.

Diagram:

1. Clinical depression
2. it (referring to clinical depression)
3. It (referring to clinical depression)
4. It (referring to clinical depression)

Source：99 年專門職業及技術人員普通考試，導遊人員、領隊人員考試試題

範例2 **Sequential progression: the themes are always different and come out of the comment of the previous sentence**（主題不同，且主題來自前一句的意見）

(1) Skillful composers have long used **silence** to build a sense of anticipation. (2) Some of **music's finest moments** are spent in transition-waiting, in essence, for the other shoe to drop. (3) The **snapshots** of this pause may have implications beyond concert halls. (4) They shine a light into what neuroscientists call "**segmentation processes**"-the techniques used by the brain to take a stream of sensory information and parcel it up into more easily comprehended pieces.

Diagram:

1. silence
2. music's finest moments
3. snapshots
4. segmentation processes

Source：101 年公務人員高等考試一級暨二級考試試題

範例3 Extended parallel progression: a parallel progression temporarily interrupted by a sequential progression

（平行的行進方式，暫時穿插順序的行進方式）

(1) When drawing human figures, children often make the head too large for the rest of the body. (2) A recent study offers some insights into this common disproportion in children's illustrations. (3) As part of the study, researchers asked children between 4 and 7 years of age to make several drawings of men. (4) When they drew front views of male figures, the size of the heads was markedly enlarged. (5) However, when the children drew rear views of men, the size of the heads was not so exaggerated. (6) The researchers suggest that children draw bigger heads when they know they must leave room for facial details. (7) Therefore, the odd head size in children's illustrations is a form of planning ahead and not an indication of a poor sense of scale.

Diagram:

1. the head too large
2. some insights
3. several drawings of men
4. front views
5. rear views of men
6. facial details
7. odd head size

Source：94 年臺大碩士班入學考題

範例4

(1) The Nobel Peace Center is located in an old train station building close to the Oslo City Hall and overlooking the harbor. (2) It was officially opened on June 11, 2005 as part of the celebrations to mark Norway's centenary as an independent country. (3) It is a center where you can experience and learn about the various Nobel Peace Prize Laureates and their activities as well as the remarkable history of Alfred Nobel, the founder of the Nobel Prize. (4) In addition, it serves as a meeting place where exhibits, discussions, and reflections related to war, peace, and conflict resolution are in focus. (5) The Center combines exhibits and films with digital communication and interactive installations and has already received attention for its use of state-of-the-art technology. Visitors are welcome to experience the Center on their own or join a guided tour. (6) Since its opening, the Nobel Peace Center has been educating, inspiring and entertaining its visitors through exhibitions, activities, lectures, and cultural events. (7) The Center is financed by private and public institutions.

Diagram:

1. The Nobel Peace Center
2. It
3. It
4. it
5. The Center
6. the Nobel Peace Center

7. The Center

Source：101 年大學指考

範例5

(1) Feeling as if you are being watched? (2) You probably are. (3) The Transportation Security Administration (TSA) in the United States recently began rolling out a new security program, Screening Passengers by Observation Techniques (SPOT), at dozens of airports around the country. (4) Using behavioral profiling, SPOT aims to identify "high-risk individuals" by monitoring passengers' body language. (5) Under this initiative, "behavior detection officers" are trained to recognize involuntary gestures, subtle facial twitches, and changes in vocal pitch that signal stress or deceit. (6) A passenger displaying suspicious behavior is taken aside for additional screening.

Diagram:

1. feeling
2. you
3. SPOT
4. high-risk individuals
5. behavior detection officers
6. a passenger

Source：101 年公務人員特種考試，外交領事人員、外交行政人員考試試題

範例6

(1) Educational researchers have identified four distinctive learning styles used by students who are attempting to master new information and concepts. (2) First, some students prefer auditory learning. (3) They learn best from lectures, tapes recordings, and class discussions. (4) The second of these styles is tactile learning. (5) This is a learning-by-doing approach, which involves such things as dissecting animals to handle their internal organs rather than reading about them. (6) Still other students are best suited to experiential learning. (7) Making use of all their senses, such as a field trip to a forest when studying botany, is the best way for these learners to understand new material fully. (8) The last of these styles is visual learning. (9) The student who favors this style relies heavily on what can be seen-books and charts, for instance-to acquire knowledge. (10) Of these four learning styles, none is considered best; but rather they are descriptive of techniques individuals use to learn effectively.

Diagram:

1. four distinctive learning styles
2. auditory learning
3. lectures, tapes recordings, and class discussion
4. tactile learning
5. learning-by-doing approach
6. experiential learning
7. senses

8. visual learning
9. what can be seen
10. they (referring to four learning styles)

Source：101 年公務人員特種考試，外交領事人員、外交行政人員考試試題

【第六章】

做筆記的策略

前言

英諺有云：A picture is worth a thousand words.（一張圖畫勝過千言萬語）。複雜的想法可以透過一張簡單的圖像或圖畫予以傳達。這也意味著視覺化的目標之一，就是可以很迅速地吸收大量資料。除此之外，人類大腦對於圖像或圖畫的記憶比文字還要持久。

有效閱讀有三步驟，第一是接觸（exposure），第二是複習（review），第三則是練習（practice）。一般而言，如果學生課後沒有再複習或練習的話，所習得的知識大多只停留於大腦的短期記憶區，很快就會忘記。若能採行上課前預習、上課時注意聽講、下課後儘快複習並多加練習，如此按部就班所習得的知識才有可能存於腦中的長期記憶區。研究顯示，上課後七天之內，學生若複習三次，可記得 80% 的內容；複習二次，可記得 70% 的內容；複習一次，大約可記得 40% 的內容；若沒有複習，則只能記得 10% 的上課內容。

根據研究，記憶分為短期記憶（short-term memory）與長期記憶（long-term memory）。短期記憶就是在腦中擁有的少數的資訊，只存在短暫時間（大約 20-30 秒）而且很容易忘記。短期記憶的容量是 7 ± 2 elements（chunks），換言之，每人短期記憶的記憶容量大約是五至九個成分、項目或區塊。相對的，長期記憶在結構上與功能上不同於短期記憶，長期記憶中項目之間的聯想可以儲存在腦中。因此，我們若將文字轉化成圖像與文字的連結，則容易將文字儲存於腦中的長期記憶區中。

以下用一個圖像說明美國學者 Professor Stephen Krashen 於 1980 年代所提出的一個情感濾網假說（Affective Filter Hypothesis）。這個假說的主要內容，是說一個語言學習者的情感因素（如動機、自尊心、自信心、焦慮）會決定其語言學習是否成功。教師應創造理想的語言學習環境，讓學習者學習動機高（high motivation）、自尊心高（high self-esteem）、自信心高（high self-confidence）而焦慮感低（low anxiety），如此一來語言可理解的輸入（comprehensible input, 下圖最左端）就可穿過情感濾網（下圖左二），到達語言習得機制（LAD, Language Acquisition Device，又稱腦中的 little black box，下圖中間），成為習得知識（下圖右二），經過了監控機制，最後成為語言的輸出（output，下圖最右端）。反之，當語言學習者學習動機低（low motivation）、自尊心低（low self-esteem）、自信心低（low self-confidence）而焦慮感高（high anxiety）時，情感濾網升高，就會阻擋語言可理解的輸入。總之，情感濾網可視為一種心智的障礙物（mental block）或心理的語言障礙（psychological language barrier），它會妨礙語言輸入到達語言學習者的語言習得機制（Krashen, 1985, p.100）。由下圖來理解此假說可說是一目了然。

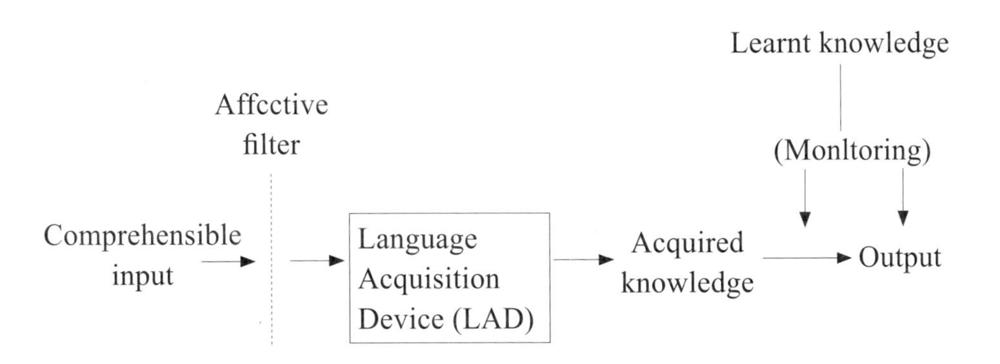

The Input Hypothesis Model of L2 learning and production (adapted from Krashen, 1982, pp.16 and 32; and Gregg, 1984)

做筆記的策略

一、康乃爾筆記法（Cornell Note-taking Strategy）

在閱讀時，如何吸收重要的資訊且完整精確的做筆記，是需要多加練習的。筆記要能促進學習的效率，才能算是好的筆記。以下介紹康乃爾筆記法，此方法的要點是將筆記本劃分為三等分（如下表）：左邊的三分之一用來記載「主標題」，第一列是主題，第二列記載關鍵字與問題；右邊的三分之二用來記載「次標題」，可以有層次的記載（如 I, II, III, IV）例如：第一行是日期與頁碼，第二行記載簡短的筆記，第三行記載答案、圖表等。

Topic	**Date** page #
Keywords	Brief notes
Questions	Answers, Diagrams, etc I. A. B. 1. 2. a. b. II. A. B. 1. 2. a. b.

尺寸大小如下圖：

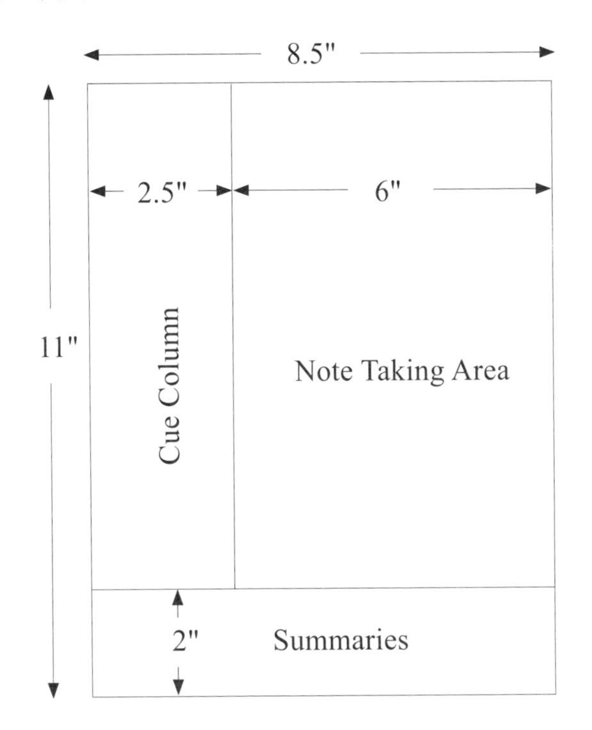

此康乃爾筆記法也可以做期刊或研討會論文的筆記，範例如下：

Paper title	**Date** **Page 1**
Abstract	– The problem under investigation – The participants or subjects – The experimental methods – The findings – The conclusions and the implications or applications
Introduction	– Establishing a research territory – Creating a niche – Occupying a niche
Literature Review	– Organization by author – Organization by theme

	– Present Tense – Past Tense – Present Participle Tense
Research Methods	– Research Design – Participants and Instruments – Data Collection Procedures – Data Analysis
Results	– Result 1 – Result 2 – Result 3
Discussion	– Discussion 1 – Discussion 2 – Discussion 3
Conclusion	– Conclusion – Limitations – Implications – Suggestions / Recommendations for Future Research

以下為語用學（Pragmatics）筆記的實例，提供讀者參考：

Pragmatics	**October 18, 2006** **p. 1**
I. Definition	The study of how language is used to communicate within its situational context.
II. Implicature	An utterance can imply a proposition (i.e., a statement) that is not part of the utterance and that does not follow as a necessary consequence of the utterance. e.g., John: Uncle Chester is coming over for dinner tonight. Mary: I guess I'd better hide the liquor.

	Entailment: A necessary consequence of an utterance is called an entailment.
	Conversational Maxims A. Maxim of Quantity: A participant's contribution should be informative. e.g., Kenny: What are you reading? Tom: A book. B. Maxim of Quality: A participant's contribution should be true. e.g., An undergraduate: Reno's the capital of Nevada. Instructor: Yeah, and London's the capital of New Jersey. C. Maxim of Relation: A participant's contribution should be relevant. e.g., Husband: What time is it? Wife: Well, the paper's already come. D. Maxim of Manner: A participant's contribution should be clear. e.g., Mr. Jones: Let's stop and get something to eat. Mrs. Jones: Okay, but not M-c-D-o-n-a-l-d-s. Exercise A: You ask a friend *Do you know where Billy Bob is?* The friend responds with *Well, he didn't meet me for lunch like he was supposed to*. a. Which of Grice's maxims does your friend's statement appear to flout? Answer: relation b. What is the implicature raised by your friend's statement? Answer: He does not know where Billy Bob is.
III. Speech Acts	A. Classification of Illocutionary Acts

	B. Felicity Conditions
	C. Illocutionary Acts (what is done) 1. Explicit versus Nonexplicit Illocutionary Acts 2. Direct versus Indirect Illocutionary Acts
	D. Locutionary Acts (what is said) 1. Expressed versus Implied Locutionary Acts 2. Literal versus Nonliteral Locutionary Acts graph, diagram
	E. Overview of Speech Act Theory
IV. Summary	The theory of pragmatics makes use of such concepts as implicature and conversational maxims (quantity, quality, relation, and manner), speech act (illocutionary and locutionary acts), a classification of illocutionary acts, felicity conditions on illocutionary acts, explicit / nonexplicit and direct / indirect illocutionary acts, and expressed / implied and literal / nonliteral locutionary acts. These theoretical constructs help explain how language users are able to use context to interpret utterances, to "do" things with words, and to "say" things without actually uttering them.

以下為 Exploring Second Language Learning 第二章筆記的實例，提供讀者參考：

I.

A.

1.

(a)

Chapter 2: Exploring Second Language Learning	**Oct. 7, 2009**
I. Contexts for language learning	A. Learner characteristics 1. Another language 2. Cognitive maturity 3. Metalinguistic awareness 4. World knowledge 5. Anxiety about speaking B. Learning conditions 1. Freedom to be silent 2. Ample time 3. Corrective feedback (grammar and pronunciation) 4. Corrective feedback (meaning, word choice, politeness) 5. Modified input
II. Behaviorism	A. Second language applications 1. Mimicry and memorization
III. The innatist perspective: Universal Grammar	A. Second language applications 1. Krashen's 'monitor model' (a) acquisition-learning hypothesis (b) monitor hypothesis (c) natural order hypothesis (d) input hypothesis (e) affective filter hypothesis
IV. Current psychological theories: The cognitivist / developmental perspective	A. Information processing B. Connectionism C. The competition model D. Second language applications: Interacting, noticing, and processing 1. The interaction hypothesis

	2. The noticing hypothesis 3. Input processing 4. Processability theory
V. The sociocultural perspective	A. Second language applications: Learning by talking
VI. Theory into practice	

二、心智圖法（Mind-mapping Strategy）

「心智繪圖」（Mind Mapping），又稱為「心智圖」（Mind Map）或概念圖（Concept Map），是英國著名的教育學家 Tony Buzan 所提出的一種嶄新的觀念與技巧。此法突破傳統的直線與線性的筆記方式，比較符合人腦樹枝狀連結法的記憶方式，這種筆記法最近在補教界與企業界非常風行，是蠻值得提倡的一種筆記法。

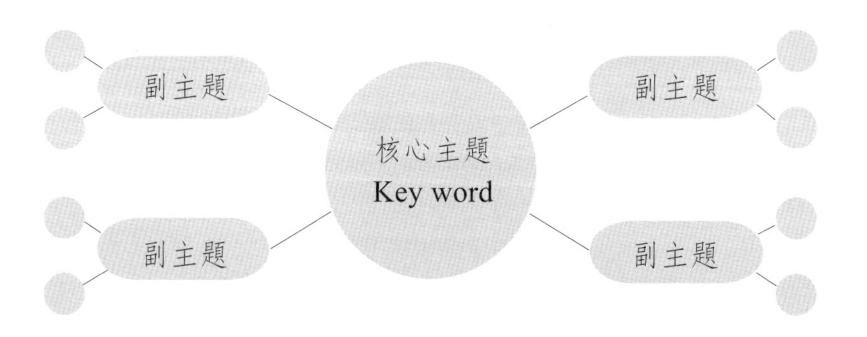

閱讀時可以利用心智圖的方式，記下文章的內容，先抓住文章重點，如此一來，筆記不但清楚也便於複習。下圖即是為了記住期刊或研討會論文內容所畫的心智圖。簡單來說，期刊或研討會論文內容可有 Introduction（序論）、Literature Review（文獻探討）、Research Methods（研究方法）、Results（結果）、Discussion（討論）、

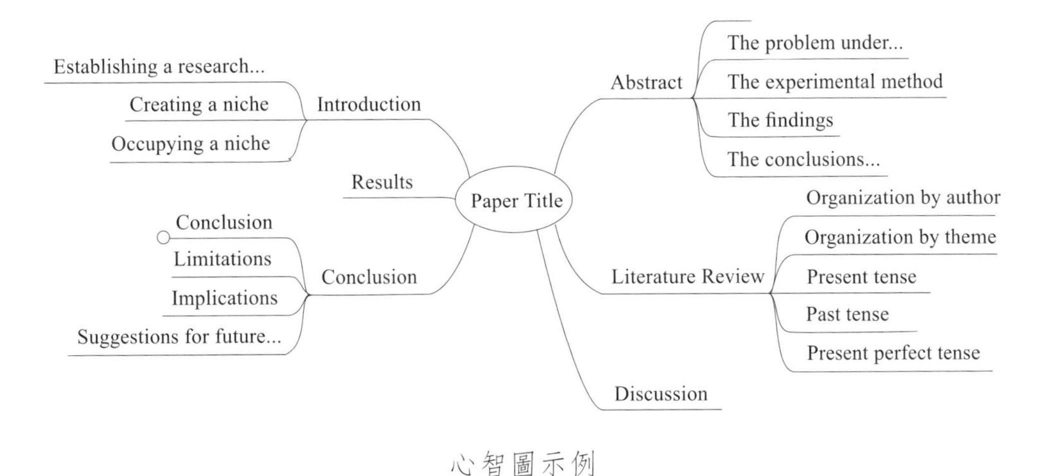

心智圖示例

Conclusion（結論）。藉著心智圖記憶法來記憶所習得的知識，是很有效率的學習方法。

三、樹狀圖法（Tree Diagram Strategy）

此圖的概念靈感來自現代語言學與認知科學之父、聞名全球的美國 MIT（Massachusetts Institute of Technology）語言學系教授 Noam

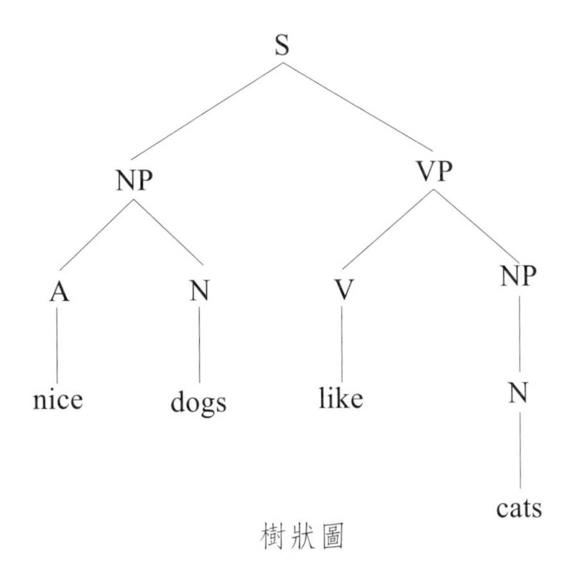

樹狀圖

Chomsky 的 Syntactic Structure Representations。

學生可利用樹狀圖的方式，記下文章的內容，先抓住文章重點，筆記簡單明瞭也便於複習。下圖即是為了記住文章內容所畫的樹狀圖。一般來說，文章內容有 Introduction（序論）、Body Paragraph 1（本文 1）、Body Paragraph 2（本文 2）、Body Paragraph 3（本文 3）、Conclusion（結論）。藉著樹狀圖記憶法來記憶所習得的文章內容，是很有效率的學習方法。

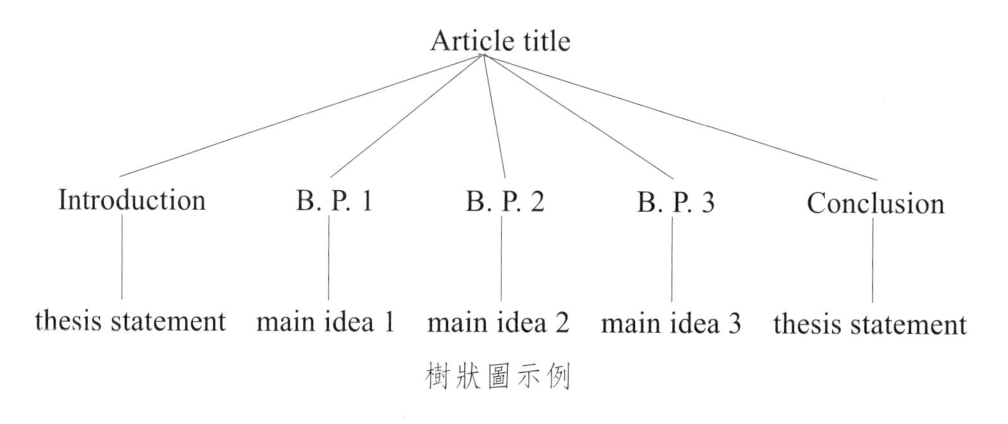

樹狀圖示例

CONCLUSION

【結語】

閱讀理解的成效取決於三個要素：第一是字彙量（vocabulary size），第二是閱讀策略（reading strategy），第三則是廣博閱讀（extensive reading）。首先，增進字彙量的方法之一，是熟悉字源學（etymology），若能掌握英文字源（即字首、字根、字尾）的邏輯性，可快速的記誦英文單字。再者，閱讀策略方面，請讀者參考本書中所提及的方法，綜合運用 top-down reading strategy （由上而下閱讀策略）、bottom-up reading strategy （由下而上閱讀策略）、interactive reading strategy （互動式的閱讀策略）或 higher-order reading strategy （高層次的閱讀策略）。最後，在廣博閱讀方面，讀者可以選擇較輕鬆的讀物，因為學理與中外實證研究顯示，「悅讀」（reading for pleasure, reading for fun）的效果最好。

閱讀是需要學習的，許多專家學者都持相同的看法。編者殷切希望以上的教學經驗與心得，能有助於提升學生的英文閱讀效率。學生若能藉由廣博閱讀（extensive reading）、密集閱讀（intensive reading）、專門閱讀（specific reading），配合上述的讀書三步驟，即接觸教材、複習該方法、練習該方法，如此一來所閱讀的資訊與知識將會存於腦海中的長期記憶區，才能提升閱讀的效果。除此之外，學生若能善用本書所介紹的高效率閱讀策略進行閱讀，則有助於提升高層次的思考力，以因應知識經濟時代的多重挑戰。

參考資料

REFERENCES

◎洪蘭（2012）。**大腦與閱讀**（原著 Reading in the Brain by Stanislas Dehaene）臺北：信誼基金出版社。

◎柯華葳、幸曼玲、陸怡琮、辜玉旻（2010）。**閱讀理解策略教學手冊**。臺北：教育部。

◎Benjamin S. (1984.) Bloom *Taxonomy of educational objectives*. Boston: Allyn and Bacon. Retrieved from http: // www.coun.uvic.ca / learning / exams / blooms-taxonomy.html

◎Grabe, W. (2009). *Reading in a second language: Moving from theory to practice*. New York: Cambridge University Press.

◎Kald, M. Nilsson, F. & Rapp, B. (2000). On Strategy and Management Control: The Importance of Classifying the Strategy of the Business. *British Journal of Management 11*, 197-212.

◎Kaplan, R. (1966). Cultural thought patterns in intercultural education. *Language Learning*, 16, 1-20.

◎Krashen, S. (1985), *The Input Hypothesis: Issues and Implications*. New York: Longman.

◎Larsen-Freeman, D. (2000). *Techniques and Principles in Language Teaching*. New York: Oxford University Press.

◎Stern, H. H. (1996). *Fundamental concepts of language teaching*. Toronto: Oxford University Press.

◎Wells, G. (1999). *Dialogic inquiry: Toward a sociocultural practice and theory of education*. New York: Cambridge University Press.

國家圖書館出版品預行編目資料

高效的英文閱讀力／彭登龍著. ——初版.——臺北市：五南, 2013.08
面； 公分
ISBN 978-957-11-7177-7（平裝）
1.英語 2.讀本
805.18 102011857

1AH0

高效的英文閱讀力

作　　者— 彭登龍
發 行 人— 楊榮川
總 編 輯— 王翠華
主　　編— 朱曉蘋　溫小瑩
責任編輯— 吳雨潔
封面設計— 吳佳臻
出 版 者— 五南圖書出版股份有限公司
地　　址：106台北市大安區和平東路二段339號4樓
電　　話：(02)2705-5066　　傳　　真：(02)2706-6100
網　　址：http://www.wunan.com.tw
電子郵件：wunan@wunan.com.tw
劃撥帳號：01068953
戶　　名：五南圖書出版股份有限公司
台中市駐區辦公室/台中市中區中山路6號
電　　話：(04)2223-0891　　傳　　真：(04)2223-3549
高雄市駐區辦公室/高雄市新興區中山一路290號
電　　話：(07)2358-702　　傳　　真：(07)2350-236
法律顧問　林勝安律師事務所 林勝安律師
出版日期　2013年8月初版一刷
定　　價　新臺幣280元

凝煉知識品味閱讀

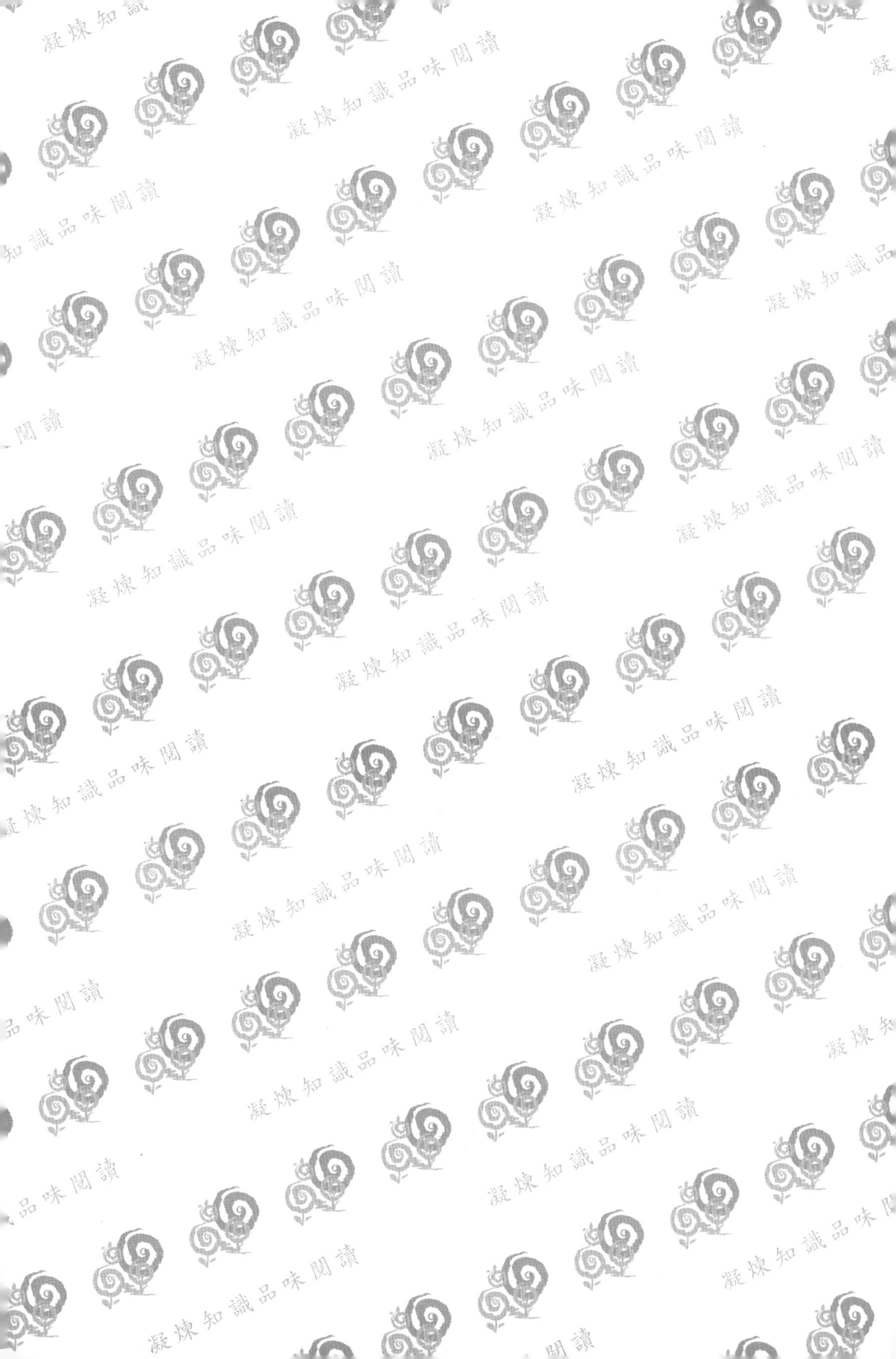